—by—

Memphis P

Nora
Maybe
a Ghost Story

Nora
Maybe
a Ghost Story

Constance C. Greene

Browndeer Press
Harcourt Brace and Company
San Diego   New York   London

Library of Congress Cataloging-in-Publication Data
Greene, Constance C.
    Nora: maybe a ghost story/Constance C. Greene.—1st ed.
        p. cm.
    "Browndeer Press."
    Summary: Nora, thirteen, and her younger sister, Patsy,
are upset that their father plans to remarry and that they like
the same boy. Amid the emotional turmoil, Nora alone feels
the presence of their mother, who died three years earlier.
    ISBN 0-15-277696-6 (hc.)
    ISBN 0-15-276895-5 (pbk.)
    [1. Sisters—Fiction.   2. Mothers and daughters—Fiction.
3. Fathers and daughters—Fiction.   4. Remarriage—
Fiction.]
    I. Title.
    PZ7.G8287No   1993
    [Fic]—dc20   92-44929

Designed by Lydia D'moch

First edition
A B C D E

Printed in Hong Kong

For Linda Zuckerman,
with love and thanks.

—C. C. G.

One

OUR FATHER might get married again soon. Patsy says she won't go. She says even if he drags her, kicking and screaming, she won't go. She says if she *does* go, if he makes her go to the church, she'll make a scene. Patsy used to be famous for her scenes. She'd go limp and collapse in a heap on the nearest tarmac. Then she'd lie there squalling like a scalded cat if she still didn't get her way.

When she did that, I'd turn my face away, pretending she wasn't my sister. I guess she did it to get attention, but I have always hated to have people stare at me.

When Patsy was really little, she pulled one of her scenes at the children's museum and Daddy turned her over his knee and smacked her bottom. I kind of liked that. I clapped, I remember.

Patsy and I are what my grandmother calls Irish twins; not quite a year apart. Patsy just turned twelve and I'll be thirteen next month. I'd die before I'd carry on in public the way Patsy does. Or did. She's improved. Our father says she must get her penchant for making scenes from Baba, our mother's mother. Baba was, and still is, an actress. She starred in a local little theater production of *Auntie Mame* last year and got rave reviews. Baba also starred in a movie once, years ago when she was young and foolish, she told us. Patsy says she bets anything Baba starred in a skin flick.

She really is outrageous, Patsy is.

Our mother died almost three years ago. She had cancer. She died at home, the way she wanted. She knew she was going to die. Her hair fell out and she got so thin her cheeks were hollow and her eyes huge.

She was beautiful, even then.

First she had one breast removed, then

the other. As if that wasn't bad enough, losing both breasts didn't do any good. She died anyway.

"Don't cry, little Nora," my mother had said to me. "I will always be with you in spirit and love you. You are my life and my joy, you and Patsy and Daddy. Please don't cry."

If she *could* be with me in spirit, I'd like to know.

Your chances of getting breast cancer increase if your mother or aunt had it. I thrust the thought from my head every time it pops in.

Patsy has breasts. Hers are bigger than mine. We don't discuss the reason our mother died. We talk about her all the time, though. We pretend she's still here. We keep her alive that way.

"I'm telling Mom, Nora!" Patsy yells when I do something she doesn't like. "You're gonna get it. She'll kill you!"

"Go wash your face," I say in a fierce imitation of Mother's voice. "Children don't wear earrings and eye shadow to school. Not in this house they don't."

Even as a kid Patsy was always trying to skin out of the house all done up like a gypsy queen. Mother would nab her and make her wash her face and take off all the jewelry.

The voice is the hardest to bring back. I can remember how Mother laughed, how she smelled. Lots of things she said. But the voice is the hardest.

The night Daddy told us he might be getting married, you should've heard Patsy.

"Mrs. Ames is going to Hong Kong next month on business," he said. "If I can get away, I'm going to join her."

Patsy pushed back her chair noisily. "May I please be excused?" she said. "I have to go to the bathroom."

"Sit down, Patsy," Daddy said. "This won't take long."

Patsy sat, but only just. She balanced her behind on the edge of her chair and jiggled to prove she really *did* have to go.

"I am going to ask her to marry me," Daddy said.

Patsy put her head on the table, as if she was fainting. I held my breath.

"Have some water, Patsy," Daddy said. "I'm not quite through."

Patsy raised her head. "What if she won't marry you?" she asked, eyes glittering. "Suppose she says no? Suppose she's been married so many times she's bored with getting married? What then?"

I stole a look at Daddy's face. He looked old. His mouth was a thin line, and I knew he was holding onto his temper with an effort.

"She has been married and divorced once," he said. "You know nothing about her. If you knew her, you might like her. Nora," he turned to me, "what have you to say? How do you feel about this?"

"I don't know," I mumbled. It was the truth.

"I would like your opinion. Patsy has given hers, in a manner of speaking. You must have some feelings, some ideas on the subject."

I could feel Patsy's hot eyes burning

holes in me. "Oh, she has plenty of ideas, Daddy," she said. "You oughta hear her."

"Silence!" Daddy thundered. He doesn't thunder very often, but when he does, he does a first-class job. "Let Nora talk."

"Well," I said, "if you want to marry her, you want to marry her, I guess. I don't know her very well so I really can't say."

Patsy burped. It was only a little burp, but I heard her.

"I want you both to know that Mrs. Ames never would take your mother's place," Daddy said stiffly. "No one could. She knows that and wouldn't even try."

"Oh, sure," Patsy said under her breath.

"I've not been very happy since your mother died," Daddy said.

I put out my hand to touch his. "How about when we hiked up the mountain last fall? And how about when we went fishing on the lake in Vermont? And when we went to the county fair? I thought you were pretty happy then," I said. "You acted happy."

"Well, yes, of course," Daddy said. "And we'll have lots more happy times, all of us. But I've found someone to love who loves me. And you won't always be here, don't forget."

"We really *want* you to get married again, Daddy," I said.

"We just don't want you to marry 'The . . .' " Patsy stopped just in time. "Marry *her*," she said. We call her "The Tooth." If you saw her, you'd know why.

"If I waited until I found someone who you two would put your stamp of approval on," Daddy said, "I might be a very old man."

First time Daddy brought The Tooth to the house, she stood in front of our mother's portrait and said in the phoniest voice, "Oh, Sam, she's lovely, so ethereal."

Patsy and I exchanged looks.

Later she topped it by exclaiming at length about our napkins, which we brought out along with the chicken casserole from Glorious Grub, the local caterer. "Oh, what beautiful double damask napkins!" The Tooth went on and on. As if the napkins were made of solid gold or something.

"They were our mother's," I said in a cold voice. "She had excellent taste."

And all the time she was there, her eyes were slipping and sliding around the house, checking everything out.

We decided she was a fool who never said what she really meant.

"She's an old witch," Patsy said in a rush. "That's why I don't like her!"

"You may go, Patsy," Daddy said. "Leave the table, please."

Patsy left. She sat on the stairs behind Daddy and made faces at me. She always does that. She used to make me giggle so much I almost threw up. I have never been sent from the table.

I chewed every mouthful thoughtfully and stared at the wallpaper in the dining room as if I'd never seen it before. It was blue and white, to match Mother's favorite china. Flower prints hung on the walls. I

remember when Daddy gave them to her.
It was the last Christmas before she died. It
was a pretty room, I thought. My favorite
in the whole house.

"Things seldom go as planned," Daddy
said. "Better not to plan, I think."

He didn't expect an answer, so I didn't
give one. Even if I'd had one, I would've
stayed silent. I cleared the table and loaded
the dishwasher.

"I'm going to do my homework now,"
I told him. "Are you all right?" He patted
me absentmindedly and said, "Go along,
Nora. You're a good child."

I went upstairs. "You really blew it," I
said to Patsy, who was now sitting on her
bed painting her toenails black. They'd had
a big sale on black nail polish down at Ma-
goon's Variety Store. Patsy bought two
bottles.

"Why'd you have to go and call her a
witch?"

"Listen—he's just lucky I didn't call
her the real word," Patsy said fiercely. "If

I'd said 'bitch,' do you think he'd have grounded me?"

"Probably," I said.

"If Mother heard what you said to Daddy last night," I said to Patsy the next day when we got home from school, "she'd wash your mouth out with soap. She'd be furious." I'd been thinking all day about it and knew she'd hurt Daddy's feelings. She shouldn't be allowed to get away with that talk, I thought.

"Yeah, well, she'd be plenty furious if she knew Daddy was thinking of marrying The Tooth," Patsy said. That's the name Patsy gave her. Her real name is Wynne. She has this fantastic overbite. Even when her mouth is closed, her teeth peek out. We can't figure out how Daddy kisses her without getting bitten.

"She doesn't fool me with that sweetsy, cutesy routine about how adorable we are —all that crap she puts out," Patsy glowered. "She doesn't mean a word of it. She knows we hate her, too. Just wait until she hooks Daddy. Just wait. When that happens, she'll start to think of ways to get rid of us.

"Well," Patsy drew herself up to her full five feet five and one half inches and thrust out her bust. (That's what we call it when she thrusts it out, Patsy's "bust.") "Two can play at that game. We eliminate *her* before she eliminates *us*," Patsy told me. "She's very jealous because she knows Daddy loves us best. She knows he'll never love her the way he loved Mother, the way he loves us, and that drives her bonkers. *If* he loves her at all, which I doubt."

"Oh, Patsy!" I wailed, suddenly overcome. "We can't let her marry him. She'd be his wife for the rest of our lives! We've got to stop him!"

Patsy put her chin in her hands and thought hard.

"We could hire an assassin," she said glumly. "To blow her away."

"Yeah, right."

"No, too expensive," Patsy said, as if she knew. "How about we go the poisonous mushroom route? It's cheaper and there wouldn't be any witnesses. In all the stories I've read, the assassin always squeals. But with the mushrooms, they don't talk. We whip up a little poisonous mushroom omelet for lunch, invite her over, feed it to her with a glass of white wine and a salad. *Perfecto.*" Patsy kissed her fingers. "She'd never know what hit her."

Then, without warning, Patsy burst into tears. She grabbed a pair of scissors from the table and waved them around her head.

"I do not want this person to be our stepmother!" Patsy said. "You dig? Do I make myself clear? I do not want her, and I will not permit her to marry our father."

I put one arm around her. Patsy might be bigger than me, but she's still my little sister and I have tried to be a mother to her since our mother died. It isn't easy.

"Maybe it'll be all right, Pats," I told her. "We can always go live with Baba and visit Daddy on weekends."

"No!" Patsy roared, leaping from my grasp. "I'm not giving up! This is our house and we're staying right here. She's not forcing us out, and that final." She pulled her shirttail out and scrubbed the tears from her face.

Patsy poked her scissors at me. "Want me to cut your hair? I feel like cutting hair."

Sometimes it calms Patsy to cut my hair. "Okay," I said. I actually needed a haircut anyway and Patsy's a very good haircutter. She leaned close to me, smelling strongly of toothpaste. (Patsy brushes her teeth four times a day and also flosses, as she says she does not want to get gingivitis and receding gums. Having a retainer is bad enough, she says.)

"I tell you this, Norrie, and you can quote me," she said. "If she thinks I'm calling her 'Mother,' she can just go suck eggs."

Two

"JUST DON'T GO HAYWIRE, okay?" I said. We went into the bathroom, and I put down the lid of the toilet seat and sat on it. Patsy began snipping away furiously, pushing my head down so my chin rested on my chest, what there was of it. I could feel the cold blades of the scissors against my scalp. Sometimes Patsy gets carried away, and I could—and once did—wind up looking like a zonked-out punk rocker or a street urchin in an Italian movie.

Patsy cuts her own hair sometimes. Last year she gave herself one of those super-sophisticated asymmetrical haircuts where one side is short and the other side sort of swoops down and around and drags your head with it so you wind up looking half-witted in a kind of sexy way.

I could never get away with that kind of haircut, but on Patsy it looked sensational. Baba said it made her look wanton.

"I thought 'wanton' was some kind of Chinese soup," Patsy had said.

"Look it up," said Baba.

Patsy's a dirty blond and I'm a mud brunet. She has gorgeous thick hair that swings. I'm getting a henna rinse one of these days to bring out the highlights that might be lurking in my hair.

"Who says she wants you to call her 'Mother' anyway?" I said in a muffled voice.

"Sit still!" Patsy hissed.

"I only want to see the tips of my ears," I said meekly. "Don't skin me bald, please."

"The tips of your ears! Gawd, what do you want to see *them* for? Did I ever tell you your ears remind me of fungus growing on the sides of your head?" Patsy asked me, knowing the answer perfectly well.

"Yeah, lots of times," I said.

"Old fungus ears, that's you," Patsy said. "Sit still and I'll turn you into a regular cheerleader type." Patsy smiled. "And we all know what *they* look like, don't we!"

Cutting my hair gives Patsy a feeling of power, I've decided. The more she cuts, the weaker I become, the further under her spell I fall, like something out of the Bible, sort of.

Finally, she stood back, admiring her work.

"Super!" she cried. "You look absolutely super!" I get nervous when she gets that enthusiastic. It's a bad sign.

"Let me see," I said. I snuck my hand around to see how much she'd taken off the back and she hollered "Whoa!" and yanked my hand away.

"If you were a real haircutter and I was a real customer," I said, "you wouldn't dare do that. I'd sue."

"If I was a real haircutter, you couldn't afford me," Patsy said. "I am ze great Sebastian, cutter to ze stars. When I cut ze hair, she stays cut."

She plonked a soap dish in my lap and said, "For ze tip. For ze folding money. I do not like ze sound of small change, you dig?"

Actually, my hair didn't look half bad.

"Put it on my account, Sebastian," I said. "I'm so rich I never carry money with me. I just charge it." I fluffed up the back of my hair and flicked my eyelashes at her. I looked like a mysterious stranger, I thought, not displeased. A sexy, mysterious stranger with an interesting past.

Patsy and I don't look anything alike. She looks like Daddy and I resemble Mother's family. A thought I hug to my heart. We're very different in temperament, too. I think things through. Patsy jumps right in. I get better marks than she does, but boys call her up and ask her places. They think she's the older one. Daddy says she's too young to start dating.

Last week Chuck Whipple, new boy in town and already a local sex symbol, called Patsy and asked her to go to a rock concert over in Stamford. His brother was driving, Chuck said.

Daddy said she could go if she was home by dinnertime. He thought the concert was in the afternoon.

Well. Talk about scenes!

Patsy stayed home and sulked.

"It is ze work of art," Patsy said, stalking me from behind. "Ze . . ."

The doorbell interrupted. Patsy crept to the window and peered out.

"Oh, my gawd!" she whispered. "It's him. I'm outta here, Nor. Keep him talking. Tie him up if you have to. I'll be back in a flash."

Patsy bolted.

Three

"HEY." Chuck Whipple ducked his head and smiled shyly down at his feet. Oozing sex appeal the while. I guess he can't help it, oozing sex appeal like that. I wonder if it gets sort of boring, though.

"Patsy home?"

"Nope. Well, maybe," I said.

I admired his dark curly hair and his long eyelashes. He had a cute nose and big ears. What the heck, you can't have everything.

"You want to come in?"

He was already in. Upstairs, it sounded as if someone was moving the furniture around. It was Patsy, changing her outfit.

"How'd you know where we live?" I said. Chuck came from some romantic place out west. Utah or Idaho, one of those.

He blushed and his big ears turned red, I was glad to see. He was pretty cool but not as cool as he thought he was. "I was just cruising around," he said, as if that answered my question.

"How old are you?" I said.

"Fourteen," he said, blushing some more. "Are you Patsy's sister?"

"Nope. I'm the sitter," I said. Sometimes I surprise myself.

"Sitter?"

"Well," I said slowly. "Patsy gets a little, you know"—and I put a finger to my head and twirled it to show how Patsy got—"a little loco."

Patsy shot into the room. She looked really old. Seventeen, at least. She had on her new black vinyl miniskirt—guaranteed to look and smell like real leather—that Daddy hadn't seen yet, much less paid for. Her denim shirt was unbuttoned practically to her belly button.

Chuck and I both blinked. Patsy, in full flower, was awesome, even I had to admit.

"I see you met my sister, Nora," Patsy said in her huskiest voice.

"Yeah," Chuck said. His eyelids flickered, but he didn't wink at me. Good thing. I never would've forgiven him if he'd winked.

The conversation limped along. Chuck had moved in during the summer and didn't know many kids. Patsy filled him in on the school, the teachers, sports, the dos and don'ts of Green Hollow. (That's where we live, Green Hollow, Connecticut. George Washington stopped here on his way to or from Valley Forge. I can't remember which. That's Green Hollow's claim to fame. I don't think he actually *slept* here; he just made a pit stop.)

I settled in on the couch with Daddy's *Wall Street Journal*. I knew Patsy wouldn't want me to hang around, but I wanted to. So I did. Patsy glared daggers at me, but then, when I didn't keel over, she pushed her charm button even harder and pretended I wasn't there. The telephone rang.

Usually we fight to see who gets there first. This time I let it ring.

At last Patsy gave in and answered it. "It's Roberta for you," she said in a frosty voice.

"Take the message," I said.

"I better split." Chuck shuffled his feet and his untied shoelaces got tangled. He stayed put.

"She wants to know about Saturday night," Patsy said. "Here." She shoved the receiver at me and almost put out my left eye.

"Hey, you old bag," I greeted Roberta. "What's up? Oh, sure. I guess. You got it. Yeah, we'll be there. Dress warm. Bring lots of cash, kid. I feel lucky. See you."

I hung up.

"Roberta says the strip-poker party's on for Saturday," I relayed the message.

Chuck Whipple's Adam's apple bounced up and down.

"Where are you from, anyway?" I asked him.

"Iowa," he mumbled, heading for the door, fighting his shoelaces. "Near Des Moines."

We watched him go.

"Sheesh!" Patsy said and stalked out of the room, stiff legged as an angry dog. It was very satisfying.

When Patsy gets really crazy, she reminds me of a snapping turtle, hissing and snapping and threatening to bite. I love her dearly, but sometimes she's tough to take. She gets out of control and needs to be put in her place.

I only wish I knew exactly where her place *is*.

Four

OUR MOTHER'S PORTRAIT hangs over the living room mantel. A red shawl is draped over her shoulders, and she's looking down pensively at her hands. Her face is sad, as if she knows what lies ahead. I think of her as a happy person, someone who laughed a lot. But it's strange. In all the pictures we have of her, and in the portrait, she looks sad.

Dee Dulin painted the portrait. Dee and our mother had been friends since they were girls. On the day our mother died, Dee was the first person to come over. She came, she said, to offer her condolences. I absolutely hate that word, *condolences*.

"I forgot the nuts," Dee said, handing

us a tin of brownies she'd baked. Her eyes were so swollen with tears she could hardly see. "I forgot to put in the nuts," Dee told us twice. The three of us sat huddled together in a big chair.

"A light has gone out of our lives," Dee said, hugging us, rocking back and forth. "Your mother was a joy, a darling girl, and she will always be."

Dee blew her nose noisily into a tissue and said, "I wonder if you girls have any idea how much she loved you."

At that, I remember, Patsy lost it. She rocketed around the room barefooted, beating her fists against anything that got in her way. Dee and I sat there, watching, not doing anything to stop her. That was the best way to handle Patsy, my mother always said, just let her go.

When Patsy fell, exhausted, into Dee's lap, Dee held her as if she were a baby, patting her on the back gently.

I wouldn't have minded if Dee had held *me* like that. Nobody, not even Daddy, had held me and comforted me for quite a while.

"There, there," Dee said. "Things will get better. Not perfect, but better. You girls and your father were her life. She was a lucky woman, you know, having you all. God was good to her."

That set Patsy off again. "Big deal!" she shouted. "Big damn deal! She's dead. I don't call that lucky. If God is so great, so good and kind and loving and all, what's he doing letting her die? Just answer me that. Forget God. God can just go take a hike, as far as I'm concerned!"

Sometimes I envy Patsy. She gets out all the bad stuff by screaming and shouting and carrying on. Then she gets the hugs and attention. I keep it all in. I wish I could let go the way Patsy does, but I can't. Sometimes I get mad and think Patsy needs a good swat on the behind.

"She made me laugh," Dee said after Patsy had calmed down. "We made each other laugh. We always wound up laughing. That was part of her gift." Dee's lips quivered as she told us these things.

Patsy kicked savagely at the leg of the chair, forgetting she was barefooted.

"Ow!" she yelled. "That hurt!" She grabbed hold of her foot and hopped around, swearing.

Dee and I doubled over, laughing. We laughed until our stomachs ached, forgetting everything except how funny Patsy looked.

Patsy glared at us ferociously, then she began to laugh, too.

We were making so much noise I wasn't sure I'd heard it. Then there was a lull and it came again. It was Mother, laughing. I swear I heard her laughing. She was there. She *was*.

"*Shhh*," I said, putting my finger against my lips. "Listen." I closed my eyes. I can hear better with my eyes closed.

"What's your prob?" Patsy said.

"She's laughing," I whispered. "I heard her just this minute. She was laughing with us."

"Who?" Dee said.

"Mother. I heard her." I said.

Our mother had a very joyful laugh that made complete strangers smile when they heard it.

"Bizarro," Patsy said, rolling her eyes. "You imagined it, Nora."

"No," I said. "She was here. I did *not* imagine it. Don't tell me that."

Dee and Patsy listened very hard.

"I can't hear anything," Patsy said crossly.

"It's possible her spirit was here with us for a moment," Dee said. "How wonderful."

We sat still as stone, listening, but Mother didn't laugh again. She had gone. She didn't make a sound.

Patsy was nine and I was ten when our mother died. Baba came to stay with us until Daddy found a housekeeper we liked. Mrs. Murty was first. She watched TV and knitted while Patsy and I racketed around the house freely. We checked our closets and drawers, looking for clues to what had happened to us. Someone, Baba perhaps, had cleared out all our mother's things. Everything was gone. I couldn't even find the red shawl, though I ransacked every bureau drawer, every hiding place in the whole house.

Our mother's closet, though, still smelled of Shalimar, her favorite perfume. So while Mrs. Murty was clucking over the goings-on in *Leftover Life to Live,* Patsy and I shut ourselves in our mother's closet and cried as we took turns stuffing our feet into a pair of her black satin high-heeled shoes we found tucked away, forgotten, in a corner.

Mrs. Moseley was next. She spent most of her time on the telephone, talking to her daughter who had just had her first baby.

"Check the stool," we heard Mrs. Moseley say over and over. "Just don't forget to check the stool."

"I thought a stool was something you put your feet on," I said.

Mrs. Moseley looked at me over the top

of her glasses and said sternly, "The stool's a BM, missy."

"What's a BM?" I asked, though I knew the answer. I liked to give Mrs. Moseley a hard time.

She threw up her hands and said, "Tell your sister what a BM is, missy," to Patsy. I think she called us both "missy" because she didn't remember our names.

From then on, every time Patsy and I went to the bathroom, one of us said to the other, "Check the stool. Just check the stool." I guess you could say it was kind of our mantra.

That kind of thing kept us from freaking out.

One fine Saturday morning when Mother had been dead about a year, Patsy said, "We could ask Dee."

"Ask her what?" I said.

"If she knows anyone for Daddy to marry," Patsy said. "She has lots of friends. She might know of someone. Then we wouldn't have to have all those lousy house-keepers. I *hate* housekeepers."

"Who doesn't?" I said.

We always went to Dee's studio for tea on Sunday afternoon. We didn't have to cross any streets, just run through the fields in back of our house. Dee gave us tea and sandwiches with the crusts cut off and little cakes. It was a very festive thing. Plus, Dee's studio was a fascinating place.

"Daddy is very lonely," Patsy said practically before she bit into one of Dee's super cucumber sandwiches.

"Poor man," Dee said. She has this colorful hair, streaked with various shades of whatever paint she's been using. She uses her hair as a sort of rag to wipe her hands on. So her hair is red and green and black and sometimes yellow. Or purple.

She is a real original.

"Have you ever been married?" Patsy asked Dee.

"Once," Dee answered cheerfully. "For about thirty minutes. Long enough. I'm a loner. I like my own company. I like eating when and what I choose. I don't want any hassle about should we have pork chops or chicken. Heck with it. The truth is, I'm selfish." Dee grinned at us.

"We think Daddy should get married to somebody so he won't be so lonely," I said.

"Give him time," Dee said. "Your mother was his heart's love. There will never be anyone to replace her. Poor man, of course he's lonely. Even with you girls around. Don't worry, darlings, he'll find someone."

There we were, looking for someone for Daddy to marry. Now he's found someone and we're thinking of ways to eliminate her.

How'd we know he was going to pick a person we couldn't stand? The thing is, we really do want our father to get married again. It's just that we want him to marry someone we *like*.

I don't think that's too much to ask.

Five

THE DAYS were getting longer. It was mid-April and cold and blowy. Pretty soon daylight saving time would begin and then it would be summer. I leaned my head against one of the small stained-glass windows on either side of our front door. My mother had told us she wouldn't have bought this house if it hadn't been for those windows.

"When the sun hits them, they dance," she'd said, as if that explained it all.

Daddy came home and found me there. It was a week since he'd told us he was going to Hong Kong with The Tooth. He hadn't mentioned it again.

"Are you reasonably happy?" he said. "Your mother always claimed those windows made her happy."

"Yes, Daddy."

He brushed his hand against my cheek. He was not a hugging, kissing man, but when he touched my cheek like that, I knew he was telling me how much he loved me. He would never say it in so many words, but there it was. He loved us, Patsy and me, very much. He would lay down his life for us. I wonder if I will ever love anyone enough to lay down my life for them. If I could have saved my mother's life by dying myself, would I have had the courage? If God had said to me, "Your mother's life will be spared if you die in her place," what would I have done?

I don't know.

I have only recently begun to think of these things.

I thought Daddy was very lonely. I didn't think he would ever get over Mother's death. He said he hadn't been happy since she'd died. Maybe if he actually *did* marry The Tooth, he'd be so happy he'd forget all about Mother. And if by some fluke he didn't marry her, what *would* happen to him when Patsy and I grow up and take off, go out into the world to begin our world-famous careers as environmentalists or epidemiologists? Mothers, even. (Patsy says you won't catch her changing dirty diapers, but I think when the loud ticking of her biological clock keeps her awake nights, she might change her mind.)

"Why would he even *think* of marrying her?" Patsy and I asked each other endlessly. "She's not even good-looking!"

"She has a certain style," Patsy said reluctantly. Patsy thought she had the answer. "Two reasons," she said. "The first is sex, *S-E-X,* pure and simple."

"But Daddy's almost fifty," I said. I don't care what I read about people having sex well into their sixties and seventies. To that I say, "BS."

"BS, BS, BS." I like the way those letters roll off my tongue. If you use the letters instead of saying the word, you can get away with it.

I gave it one more "BS" for good measure. It drives Patsy nuts when I do that. I like driving her nuts.

"Daddy has his needs," Patsy said primly. "He is a gentleman of the old school. The Tooth seduced him, and now she's laying a guilt trip on him. That's what gentlemen of the old school do. They marry whoever seduces them because it's expected of them."

"Daddy is too old to be seduced," I said.

Patsy's eyebrows soared. "Who says?" Then, in that special irritating tone she uses when she's the professor and I'm the student, she said, "You have to understand, Nora. The Tooth is a woman of the world. She's also a manipulator. She knows how to manipulate men, especially. She's got Daddy painted into a corner. There's no way out except marriage. She seduced him, so Daddy figures he has to marry her to make an honest woman out of her."

"You're so full of it, you make my eyes smart," I said.

"Too bad that doesn't happen to the rest

of you," Patsy said smugly. "Plus, Daddy is good-looking in a sort of middle-aged way. He has all his hair, and he doesn't have a big gut. He makes pretty big bucks, and his manners are lovely. Baba even says so. Let's face it, if it wasn't for me and you, Norrie, he'd probably have been snapped up long ago. They take one look at us and figure 'Whoa! Who needs these two gross teen-agers? They are nothing but bad news.' Then they back off and look elsewhere."

"You're the one that's bad news," I said. "I'm a pussycat."

That night Daddy was going to be late, so Patsy and I pigged out on home fries and banana-and-bacon sandwiches. Mash a couple of really ripe bananas with a fork and mix in crisp bacon and toast the bread. A real taste treat.

We ate the sandwiches as we strolled through the downstairs, pretending to be real-estate people showing the house to pro-spective buyers.

"And this," Patsy made a swooping

gesture, "is the drawing room. We simply *live* in this room, although we do not draw here. Isn't this room done in excellent taste? It also gets the afternoon sun and can take a party of thirty or so with no sweat. And who is this lovely woman?" We stood looking at Mother's portrait, as if seeing it for the first time.

"I wonder what The Tooth's going to do about *that*?" I said. "Suppose she'll turn it to the wall? Or banish it to the attic? Second wives should never live in the first wife's house. I've heard that's death to romance. Too many memories chill out love.

"Like in *Rebecca*. Remember, Pats? When Joan Fontaine got so freaked out about how lovely and wonderful Rebecca was that she dressed up like Rebecca's portrait and almost blew the whole thing?"

Oh, how I love that movie. It's so romantic.

Patsy pointed her one long red fingernail at me. The others are all painted black. Patsy got the one long red nail idea from some rock star. Daddy threatened to sit on her stomach and cut the nail off, but so far he hasn't.

"Know something, Nor? I wouldn't be surprised if Mother's hanging around this house, catching the vibes, checking out The Tooth's undies."

A month ago Patsy and I discovered the bottom drawer in our guest room seething with The Tooth's lingerie.

"How dare she!" Patsy shrieked, waving a filmy bra and a silk nightgown in my face. "How dare she! Does this mean she plans on coming again? What exactly does leaving your underwear in a strange bureau drawer mean? Think on it, my love."

"Remember Louise," I said.

Louise had been our baby-sitter. We loved her. She's married now, with a baby of her own. After Mother died Louise taught us practically everything we know about life, love, and the battle of the sexes. I guess she thought it was her duty. One of the bits of info Louise dished out was to always leave an article of clothing, like an earring or a scarf or a stray shoe, in a boy's car or pocket, if necessary, so he'll have to call you to tell you he found it and should he bring it over. Or, Louise advised, if you really like the guy and he doesn't call, you can call him and ask if he found whatever it was you left and you'd like it back. This, Louise assured us, almost always wound up with the guy asking for another date. Or maybe his older, cuter brother asking for a date, depending on the sexiness of the lost article. Once, Louise said, she'd tucked a pair of bikini panties with big red lips printed on them under the passenger seat and she got three calls, including one from the date's father.

"Damn straight I remember Louise!" Patsy roared, dumping The Tooth's undies in a pile on the floor. She was threatening to torch them, but I stopped her. Instead, we stuffed everything into a paper bag and put it in the Goodwill drop box at the A&P.

We waited for The Tooth to inquire about the whereabouts of her undies, but she never said a word. She knew. She was too smart to ask, though. Too cagey. She was playing a waiting game, Patsy and I decided.

Was Mother hanging around, as Patsy had said?

"And if our mother *is* hanging around," Patsy went on, "and you really *did* hear her laughing that time, she knows what's going on. She knows about The Tooth and everything. Maybe her spirit has returned to those she loved, and that's us, Nor. She wants to let us know she still loves us even if she is no longer here on earth."

I've thought about how I'd feel if Mother's ghost *was* roaming through the house. I might be afraid, though I don't know why. She would never harm us in any way. I want to see Mother again more than anything. There are piles of things I want to ask her, talk to her about. But I wonder.

Would she touch me, kiss me, tell me to take my feet off the glass-topped table, as she always did? All I want is for her to be free of pain and to be at peace.

Six

ROBERTA MIDDLETON has a strip-poker party every time her parents go away and leave her Aunt May in charge. Aunt May is pretty old and deaf and she likes to drink a hot toddy while she watches *Wheel of Fortune* with the sound turned up to the max. When Aunt May's in charge, the sky's the limit.

In strip poker, you're supposed to take off one piece of clothing every time you lose. I wear ten or twelve T-shirts, one over the other, when I play. Other kids wear tons of bracelets and/or earrings, which they remove slowly, one by one. That way no one ever gets down to the bare bod.

Actually, I wouldn't have minded checking out a couple bare bods belonging to Roberta and/or Erica. It was my own bare bod I didn't want to flaunt. Well, maybe *flaunt* isn't exactly the right word.

Roberta thought strip poker sounded sexy. If you ask me, playing strip poker with a bunch of girls is about as sexy as playing Go Fish or Old Maid.

Patsy and I talked it over and decided Roberta's crowd was too immature. Roberta and I had been in the same Brownie troop and Roberta says that forms an unbreakable bond. Roberta's mother was our troop leader. She's very civic minded and is on lots of committees and stuff. She's also president of the PTA and she collects for all diseases, big and small. When she walks up a person's front walk with her collection can in hand, the person inside hides. Then, after fifteen minutes or so, they peek out to see if she's gone and there she is, standing, waiting. Roberta's mother can be very patient.

Whenever I threaten to leave Roberta's crowd on account of her friends' immaturity, Roberta gets all huffy. "All right for you," she says. "After all we've been through."

"What?" I say. "Name one thing!"

"Plenty of things."

"Oh, all right." I always give in. I guess I like Roberta in spite of everything.

"Let's not go to Roberta's," Patsy said. "I'm not in the mood for juvenile high jinks."

"We can say we have to go out to dinner with Daddy and The Tooth," I said. "Remember? He wants us to go out with them Saturday night so we can get to know her better. So it wouldn't be a lie."

"Forget it," Patsy said. "So we go to Roberta's, but I swear on a stack of Bibles, it's the last time. Next time Roberta has a strip-poker bash, I'll probably have a date, anyway."

"Who with?"

"Who do you think, turkey?"

"Daddy won't let you go out on a date with a boy," I said. "You're only twelve. He might let you go, I guess, if I offered to chaperone."

That shut her up.

Roberta called. "Bring refreshments,"

she said. "My mother's all bent out of shape because she had to chair the library meeting last night and that upset her schedule. Annabelle's bringing her sinful chocolate delight—Milky Ways, chocolate chips, and Hershey Bars all melted together." Over the phone I could hear Roberta smacking her lips.

"Maybe we can't come," I said. "Daddy wants us to go out to dinner with him and The Tooth."

"Whoa, heavy duty," Roberta said. "Is it black-tie?"

She gets that stuff from her mother, who always asks "Is it black-tie?" even when someone invites her to a cookout.

In the end Patsy and I went to Roberta's. It seemed the lesser of two evils. To give you an idea of Roberta's crowd, they drink tomato juice with a dash of Tabasco and call it a "Virgin Mary." (I scarcely think the Virgin Mary would've drunk tomato juice, even if they *had* tomato juice back then, which I doubt.)

Patsy and I made our world-famous

yogurt dip to bring to Roberta's. It's cut-up radishes and cucumbers and anything else you have handy added to plain yogurt with a splash of salsa, medium hot. Everybody hates it except us. It makes your mouth tingle.

Roberta came to the door wearing a jumpsuit covered with gigantic red flowers. She is a large, stout girl with a booming voice who should never be caught dead wearing a jumpsuit, with or without red flowers. This is only my private opinion.

"I just got the skinny on the invaders," Roberta said, dragging us inside. Roberta always drags her guests inside as if she's afraid they might escape.

"Word got out about this party." Roberta's eyes darted from me to Patsy and back to me. "Zero hour is eight P.M. That's when the enemy plans to attack. Even as we speak, the troops are gathering."

The last time Roberta threw a strip-poker party, some guys we knew tried to crash. So Roberta got out her father's bullhorn, a souvenir of his unsuccessful bid to be elected town supervisor, and turned on the enormous outdoor spotlight designed to scare off would-be burglars, and trumpeted, "STOP RIGHT THERE! FREEZE!"

At the same time a bunch of us set off some rockets left over from the Fourth of July and watched those bozos run like thieves.

It was fun.

"Where's your aunt?" I said. I could hear the TV blaring from behind closed doors.

"She's zoned out watching a game show and drinking her hot toddy," Roberta said. "We're all set."

We traipsed down to Roberta's rec room. They were all there: Maura, Annabelle, and Sue, with Sue's droopy cousin Erica fresh from Boston. Erica's always telling us what her mummy says. Mummy says Boston's the culture capital of the universe. Mummy says Boston's museums, theater, ballet, and symphony, not to mention restaurants, are the best in the western world.

As we settled in, Erica was saying, "Mummy reads at least four books a week, sometimes five." Big deal.

"Has she read the sequel to *Gone with the Wind*?" I asked.

Oh yes, Mummy had devoured that one, Erica said.

"I read in the paper that that book was written at a fourth-grade reading level," I said. That was true. I *had* read that.

Erica ignored me, but Patsy gave me a smile. We cut for deal. Patsy won. She shuffled like a pro.

"Are you Egyptian?" Patsy asked Erica.

Erica looked startled. "No," she said. "Why?"

Patsy shrugged and dealt. "It's just that you're always saying 'Mummy this' and 'Mummy that,' so I thought maybe you were Egyptian."

I smiled at Patsy. Then I dealt. I gave myself three kings and a pair of aces, a full house. Keeping my poker face on, I won a big pot. I scooped up the pile of chips, maintaining my poker face, trying not to look too victorious.

Eight o'clock came and went. I wondered if Chuck Whipple was one of the troops coming to crash the party. Probably not. He was too new and too old. Too new in town and too old for the bevy of twelve- and thirteen-year-old bozos out there falling all over their own feet, getting ready to storm the battlements.

Roberta fidgeted, checking her watch every few minutes.

"It's twenty to nine," she said at last. "I guess they're not coming." Somebody, I think it was Erica, sighed.

We ate the refreshments. Maura brought cherry bread made with maraschino cherries. She always brought cherry bread.

"It tastes funny," Roberta said.

"My mom said to use Crisco instead of butter on account of cholesterol," Maura said.

Our yogurt dip was outstanding, as usual.

"That stuff's gross," Annabelle said,

stuffing her face with her own sinful chocolate delight.

I lost three hands in a row after my big win and soon was down to my green brontosaurus T-shirt.

"Aren't you a little old for dinosaurs?" Erica said. "My little brother has a shirt exactly like yours."

"How old's your little brother?" Roberta said.

Good old Roberta.

"Four and a half," Erica said with the air of someone who's won the pot even though she's lost.

I think she was getting even.

At the stroke of ten, we split. We sprinted out of Roberta's so fast we didn't even say "Thanks for a nice time."

I had just unlocked our front door when the telephone rang. Patsy gave me one of her hip checks, which she's good at—being on the hockey team and all—and sent me flying.

"Hello," she said in that breathless way

she has that always makes people think she's been running.

"Oh, it's you! Yeah, we just got here. It was fab, all right. Positively fab. The best. Pretty much fun. See you."

Patsy hung up. "*Sheesh*, that Roberta," she said. "She is so insecure. She doesn't even give you time to get home before she's checking to see if you had a good time. She said everybody said it was the best party they'd ever been to."

"What'd you say?"

"I lied and said it was great. What the heck. If it makes her feel good, it's worth it, right?"

"Patsy," I said, in a rush of memory, imitating my mother's voice, "you simply have got to learn to tell the truth."

And Patsy, remembering, too, said "Why?"

Seven

LITTLE PIECES of memory hit when you least expect them.

It was early September five years ago and very hot. We went downtown to buy new school shoes. Patsy wanted boy's high-tops. Mother said she couldn't have them.

Mother sat on a bench in the shade on the edge of the village green while Patsy and I raced to check out the statue of the Revolutionary War soldier kneeling there with his gun on his shoulder.

Patsy patted the soldier's stone head while I went off to the war memorial, which was made of brown marble and listed the names of all the young men and boys from Green Hollow who'd died defending their country.

"Here's a James," Patsy said, putting her finger on a John. One thing she knew for sure was the letter *J*. She was just learning to read and a little slow at it.

"What's this one, Nora?" Patsy said, pointing to another name.

"Elias," I said importantly. I spelled it out for her. "*E-l-i-a-s*. E-li-as."

I was a good reader. I liked spelling out stuff for Patsy.

At the shoe store, Mr. Endorf shook hands with us. "Well, well, girls. Good to see you," he said. "You're looking nice and tan. Have a good summer?" Mr. Endorf was a nice man. We always bought our shoes at his store.

"Just sit yourselves down and I'll measure your feet, see what I have that might suit you." Mr. Endorf ran his hands through his sparse hair.

"What grade you going into, Nora?" he asked me.

"Third," I said proudly.

"Third!" Mr. Endorf's astonishment knew no bounds. His bushy black eyebrows shot up and down. "I had no idea. How time flies! How about you, Patsy?"

"I'm in third grade, too," Patsy said.

"No, you're not," I said. "You're only in second."

"Liar, liar, pants on fire," Patsy chanted. Mother made us shush and sat between us, as she always did in church, to keep the peace. Mr. Endorf measured our feet and went into the back of the store to find just the right shoes for us.

"Behave," Mother said. Patsy slid off her chair and wandered off to see what she could find. Mother and I watched as she bent down and picked up bits and pieces of things from the carpet as if she were on a beach hunting for seashells.

Mr. Endorf returned, carrying several shoe boxes under his arm.

"These are the latest thing," he said, taking out a pair of terrible brown shoes. "All the girls are wearing them."

"I hate them," Patsy called out, putting a few bits of fluff into her pocket. "I want high-tops." She skittered off toward the front of the store to check the windows.

"Try this one, Nora. This looks like the right shoe for a young lady going into third grade," Mr. Endorf said.

I walked around cautiously, looking down at my feet. I wished for a different shoe, one not so shiny, one more grown-up, with different heels, a different color. Mr. Endorf pressed down on my toe to show my mother how much growing room there was. Oh, those shoes were perfect, all right. Mr. Endorf promised they would last me until the spring, perhaps beyond. They were first-class shoes, he assured us.

I believed him. I just didn't like them much.

Then Patsy came wobbling toward us, splendid in a pair of silver high-heeled sandals she'd found left half in, half out of their box by some careless previous customer.

Oh, but they were beautiful shoes. My heart ached for them. I would like those, Mr. Endorf, I said to myself. Wrap them

up, please. I will take them. They are just
what I have always wanted.

"Careful now, Patsy." Mr. Endorf's
voice trembled. "Wouldn't want you to trip
and fall."

Patsy kept on coming, not so much as
slowing down. Without a word, our mother
got up and snatched Patsy straight out of
those silver sandals and gave her one good
shake that set Patsy's hair to dancing.

"Sit," Mother said, the way you say "Sit!"
to a dog who's been to obedience school.

Patsy sat.

"They certainly keep you hopping, don't
they?" Mr. Endorf said.

"That they do," Mother agreed.

Patsy did. I didn't.

After, she treated us to chocolate sodas
at O'Malley's. We even got extra whipped
cream. The glasses were tall and thin and
sweaty, like the boy behind the counter.
Nothing ever tasted as sweet as those chocolate sodas.

Mother had a chocolate malted. If

she'd had anything else, we would've been shocked.

"They always make me feel sick," Mother told us. She never drank a chocolate malted without saying this. "They remind me of when I was your age. Every time I drank a malted, I felt as if I were going to throw up."

"And did you?" we asked, already knowing the answer.

"Never." Mother shook her head. "Not once."

We liked that. It made us proud. How many mothers could say that?

On our way home, we ran into our mother's friend Mrs. Beatty.

"Darlings, how are you all?" Mrs. Beatty dressed like a movie star, all in red, with dangly earrings in the broad daylight and painted fingernails so long they curved under, like a bird's claws. Mrs. Beatty was dazzling beyond belief, although even at eight, I suspected she might be a little silly.

"And how are the darlings?" Mrs. Beatty

bent down to look into our faces. She was so close, I could see myself in her eyes. She smelled absolutely delicious.

"We got new school shoes," Patsy said. "I hate mine. Nora likes hers."

I stared at the pavement. *That's what you think.*

"Bless you, my angels. What grades are we going into? Nora?"

"Third," I said, wondering why everyone asked me that.

"Wonderful. And you, Patsy. What grade is it for little Patsy?"

Patsy thought it over.

"Fourth," she said in a loud voice, not looking at me.

I clapped my hand over my mouth, and Mrs. Beatty cried "Lovely! Lovely!" as if Patsy had said something very daring, very original. Her earrings did a mad dance against her cheeks as she promised to call our mother soon, after things quieted down.

"What things?" I asked.

"She's always very busy," Mother said, smiling. Then she said, "Patsy," trying not to smile. "What *am* I going to do with you? You simply have to learn to tell the truth."

"Why?" said Patsy.

Eight

"IT'S NONE OF my business, Sam, but your tires are bald," Baba said.

"Better than my head, Baba," Daddy replied. "You look smashing, darling," he said to her.

"Sam," Baba said, looking pleased. "You always were a sweet talker."

Daddy? A sweet talker? Patsy and I exchanged looks. Adult dialogue can be very revealing. I've decided no one is precisely the person they seem.

Most of Baba's friends have had little tucks taken here and there, she said.

"Tucks? Like sewing? With a needle and thread, you mean?" I said.

"When the face starts to sag, they have

tucks taken," Baba explained. "To make themselves look better. But I am as God made me," she said proudly, lifting her head and retying her pink silk scarf. "A bit of color around the face distracts the eye and also conceals wrinkles in the neck."

"God made you a handsome woman and you remain one," Daddy said. "Now let's see about the portrait."

It was Sunday. After church we went out for brunch—a special treat. When we got home Dee Dulin had asked Daddy if she could borrow Mother's portrait to hang in a one-man show she was having in a local art gallery, and Daddy had taken it down from its accustomed place. We all stood looking at the bare spot, which seemed stark and empty without it.

"What do you think, girls?" Daddy had said. "Is it all right with you?"

"It's only a loan, right, not for keeps?" I said.

"Only a loan," Daddy said.

We watched as Daddy put the portrait

against the wall with great care, as if it were made of glass. "It's a wonderful likeness," he said softly, running his hand over Mother's red shawl, her face.

"This room could stand a coat of paint," Baba said, hands on hips, lips pursed. "Gray would be nice, with a touch of green to it, perhaps. Gray's a lovely soothing color."

"I like red. How about red?" I said.

"No, yellow," Patsy piped up. "Yellow's a happy color."

"So's red."

"Later, girls," Daddy said.

"It's none of my business, Sam," said Baba, "but you really should get someone in to wash the windows. The longer you let them go, the harder it is to get them clean."

"Maybe later," Daddy said again.

"And furthermore," Baba said, "I know it's none of . . ."

"My business!" Patsy and I cried in unison.

"Girls," Daddy said sternly.

Baba pulled a hurt face. "I only want to

be of some help," she said. "Why not let me call my little man, the one who's so reasonable, and have him come out and give you an estimate, at least."

"I'm very busy at the office right now. It'll have to wait." Daddy spoke in a voice that ended the discussion.

"Far be it from me to tell you how to run your life, Sam," Baba said.

"*Ooops.*" Daddy patted his pockets. "My wallet must be upstairs." He took the stairs two at a time. We listened as he closed the door to his room, listened to the little *ping* sound the telephone makes when someone makes a call from the upstairs phone.

"How's the romance going?" Baba asked us, straightening the pillows on the couch.

"What romance?" Patsy and I said, wide-eyed. We like to tease Baba. She's extremely teaseable.

"You two are a tough lot, that's all I can say," Baba said, in a huff. "It's not as if I'm a gossip, after all. I'm your grandmother."

When Daddy came back down, he ran Baba home on the bald tires while Patsy and I started to do our homework. Baba had had her driver's license suspended, due to an excess of speeding tickets.

"You know what Daddy means when he says 'later,' I trust," Patsy said. She didn't even give me a chance to say "yes" or "no." She plunged on. "He means later, when he brings The Tooth home as his bride and carries her over the threshold. When that happens, I'm outta here."

"Where will you go?" I said.

Patsy shrugged."Maybe I'll join the army. Or the marines. Or maybe I'll sign up as an *au pair* and go to Switzerland so I can go skiing on my day off." A girl we know did that the summer she was a junior in high school.

"Yi-yi-yi," I said. Patsy skis the way Baba drives, totally out of control at all times.

"You're too young," I said. "The army doesn't want you, or the marines, either. You're only twelve."

"In the Civil War there were plenty of kids my age in uniform," Patsy said. "Drummer boys and nurses and all."

"So? Different days, different times," I said, knowing perfectly well if Patsy decided to join the army, she'd probably find a way.

I tuned Patsy out. If Daddy brought The Tooth home as our stepmother, I planned on asking Dee if I could move into her studio and be a caretaker, fix tea for her, wash out her brushes and sweep the floor, and be a general handyperson. In exchange she'd let me sleep on her beat-up couch and fix soup and stuff for me on her hot plate.

And on weekends, when Daddy was home, I'd go over and we d have cozy talks while The Tooth was out shopping. Maybe we'd even toast marshmallows. That way, I wouldn't have to see much of her, and Daddy and I could have quality time together, the way parents are supposed to have with their kids. Which means they don't see much of the kids, but when they do see them, everyone is friends. Nobody fights or shouts or is mean. Nobody pulls a scene or anything. There's nothing but love and goodwill.

I don't see anything wrong with having quality time with your father.

Suddenly, Patsy went into her Groucho Marx crouch, knees bent, eyes wild, as she staggered around the kitchen carrying an imaginary person. She slipped a dill pickle out of the jar on the table and stuck it in her mouth for a cigar. She was imitating Groucho imitating Daddy carrying The Tooth over the threshold, I knew. Tears stung my eyes.

"He better watch it," I said, "or his bad back will go out on him again."

"I bet she tips the scales at a good one-thirty or so," Patsy said. "And I'm talking *nekkid* here, Nor, nude!"

The telephone rang.

"Tell Sam when he comes in," Baba's voice said, "that I managed by a stroke of luck to reach my little man, name's Mr. Pepper, and he says he'll stop by tomorrow to give your father an estimate for the painting and the windows."

"I'll tell him, Baba," I said.

Patsy went into the dining room to set the table and I opened a can of cream of mushroom soup. Mushroom soup covers a multitude of casseroles, I've discovered. Roberta pours it on a can of tuna fish and noodles and tops the mess with crushed potato chips. She swears the crowd goes wild.

The telephone rang again.

"Hello," Chuck Whipple said.

"Oh, hi, Chuck," I said. "Just a sec. I'll get Patsy."

"That's okay," Chuck said. "I really wanted to talk to you."

"What?" I said.

Patsy was at my elbow, snapping her fingers for me to hand over the receiver.

I said "What?" again, not believing my ears.

Patsy grabbed the phone from me. "Hi, Chuck," she said. "What's up?"

I went into the bathroom and threw cold

water on my hot cheeks. I washed my hands awhile, until my fingertips began to wrinkle. I waited for Patsy to holler, "He wants to talk to you, Nora!" But she didn't.

When I came out of the bathroom, Patsy said, "I really like Chuck. He likes me, too, I can tell." She grinned at me. "Hey, Nora, I just got an excellent idea. When he asks me on another date, you talk Daddy into letting me go. Okay? Tell Daddy what a super guy Chuck is, how responsible and adult he is, all that crap. Only it's not crap. I think Chuck is responsible and adult. He's much more sophisticated than the guys around here. Maybe it's because he's from Iowa. I bet you could talk Daddy into letting me go. Please, Norrie, please, *please*." Patsy grabbed me and tried to swing me around in time to the music coming from the radio.

"Stop it," I said, close to tears. "Let me alone!"

"What's your prob?"

"And don't say 'prob,'" I said. "I hate it. The word's *problem*."

"Boy, *you* certainly are in a foul mood," Patsy said.

I went to my room, put on my night-gown, and went to bed. It was too early to go to sleep, so I lay there, thinking. I had no one to talk to. Patsy didn't have an idea in the world that I might like Chuck, too, or that he might like me. She was very wrapped up in herself, all right. She was what they call self-absorbed. I hoped she'd grow out of it. Fast.

I heard Daddy come home. He'd gone out for some cigarettes. I saw the lights of his car on the ceiling. I heard him slam the front door extra hard, making sure it was locked. Then I heard him talking to some-one. Patsy, I guess. My bedside clock said it was ten-fifteen. No, he probably was on the phone to The Tooth. It was no good, waiting for him to get off so I could talk to him. I loved him more than anyone, but after a long day he wouldn't want to listen to me talk about Chuck Whipple and how selfish Patsy was.

I lay there, thinking about breast cancer and dying, and how it must be to be in love and about Daddy getting married. It was all a jumble in my head. There were so many things to figure out, to understand, and so far, I was coming up zero on all of them. I felt alone—very, very alone.

A sudden current of air skittered across the floor like a live thing. I wasn't sure if I was awake or asleep, but I know I heard something. It could be a mouse, I thought. Mice didn't bother me. The moonlight coming in the window was pale and thin, and the curtains billowed wildly as if a high wind had come up. I hugged myself and said, "Mother."

I knew I was getting slightly loony on the subject, but I couldn't seem to stop. I pulled the covers up to my chin and, though I was getting very sleepy, I forced my eyes to stay open in case she gave me some kind of a sign she was there.

Someone sighed. Probably it was me. I sigh a lot. I thought about getting up and closing the window. Then something brushed against my forehead, something cold, on the exact spot where Mother had always kissed me good-night. Masses of whispers swirled around my head like fog.

"Sleep," the whispers seemed to say. "Sleep, sleep, sleep."

Next thing I knew, it was morning.

Nine

THE THOUGHT occurred to me even before I opened my eyes:

If ghosts returned to the ones they loved, how come Mother hadn't shown herself to Patsy? Or Daddy? Or Baba?

I think it's because I need her and they don't. Well, of course, Daddy *needs* her. We all do. I just think right now I need her more than anyone else. And she knows it. Some day I will discuss this with Daddy and Patsy and Baba. Maybe. In the meantime, I'm hanging on to Mother's ghost for dear life.

Patsy and I would like for Daddy to marry Dee. Dee and we get along very well. Dee has no children, which is a shame, as she treats children with the greatest respect and never talks down to them. This is rare in an adult with no children. Or even with. Dee loves us and we love her, so why can't Daddy love Dee, too?

Dee's studio is one of my favorite places. It is a large, light, square room. It is also very messy. Dee says it is organized chaos, which I somehow doubt. She says she knows exactly where everything is in that studio. One of the main reasons I like the studio so much is its smell. It is made up of several ingredients: paint, chalk, and turpentine. To me the smell of turpentine is very exciting. It is a kind of greasy smell that makes my nose itch. Once when I was younger, I put a dab of turpentine behind my ears when Dee wasn't looking, the way I'd seen my mother do with her Shalimar. I put a few drops on my wrists, also. And later, everywhere I went, people scrunched up their faces and sniffed and wondered out loud what it was that smelled so peculiar.

Turpentine is my Shalimar, I decided.

"You are weird, Nora, just plain weird," Patsy said when I told her what I'd done. But I think she was jealous she hadn't thought of it first. It was a Patsy kind of thing to do, which made it doubly special.

The invitation to Dee's reception at the art gallery arrived. It said Wine and Cheese Reception on Friday. Five to Seven. I was still mad at Patsy, but she didn't pay any attention so I got over it.

As usual Patsy had it all planned.

"I will wear a beret and suck on a cigarillo," she said. "I will wear my black tights and lots of eye makeup. I will drink wine and eat cheese and look at all the art stuff with narrowed eyes so people will think I know what I'm doing. They will probably think I am an artist myself."

Daddy, who was doing the crossword puzzle, which always makes him tune out the rest of the world, said, without looking up, "That's what you think, guys."

We like it when he calls us "guys." It makes him seem very young and jaunty and carefree, none of which he is. Although we have tons of snapshots of him when he was in college and he was all of those things. Back then.

Baba's little man had come and gone. When he gave Daddy his estimate on how much it would cost to paint the living room, Daddy whistled and said, "Maybe later, Mr. Pepper. I'll be in touch. Thanks for coming over."

"I will meet a tall, thin dark man with a beard," Patsy continued. "This bozo has been giving me the eye for some time. At last he speaks."

"Yeah, yeah," I said. "Turns out he wants to borrow ten bucks."

"This man is a world-famous artist whose works hang in every museum in the country," Patsy said. "He would like to paint me. In the nude, of course." She looked at me, but I refused to look back. "That's what artists do, they paint people

in the nude," Patsy said. "They think nothing of it."

"Who, the nude people or the artists?"
I asked. "I have always heard that artists'
models develop chilblains from posing in
the nude and die of malnutrition and/or
pneumonia."

"You are a killjoy, Nora," Patsy said.
"And also a pill."

Daddy looked up from his puzzle with
unfocused eyes.

"Bare *blank* choirs where late the sweet
birds sang," he said in a dreamy way. "Five
letters."

"Ruin'd," I said. The word just popped
out. "That's without the *e*." I didn't know
I knew it until I said it.

"That's from Shakespeare's sonnet, number seventy-three," I said.

"Good Lord." Daddy filled in the blank.
"It fits." I could see he was tremendously
impressed, as I was myself. So was Patsy, I
could tell.

"Where on earth did you learn that,

Nora?" Daddy himself can recite "Young Lochinvar" in its entirety, which he used to do when Mother was alive. I haven't heard him recite it since she died.

"Our English teacher Ms. Hall read us that sonnet last week," I said. "She wants us to read a sonnet by Shakespeare every night for a week. And memorize it. She says it's good discipline to memorize poetry. It's good for your brain as well as your psyche, she says."

"Well, well," Daddy said. "That is good news. I must meet your English teacher some day and compliment her."

Patsy met my eye. We were thinking the same thing. Introduce Daddy to Ms. Hall. So she's no chicken. She's nice. About sixty, maybe more, and she leans toward purple eye shadow to match her dress or her scarf or even her lipstick. She and Daddy might fall madly in love and could take turns reciting poetry to each other.

"I hope you are both free *this* Saturday," Daddy said. "I've asked Mrs. Ames to go to the dinner theater in Darien. They're do-ing *Oklahoma!*, and I think you'd enjoy it. The music is wonderful. It would be nice if you both came along. It would give you a chance to get to know her better. She's very fond of you two, you know."

Mrs. Ames, aka The Tooth.

I almost asked Daddy if he was still plan-ning to ask The Tooth to marry him, and if he was still planning on going to Hong Kong with her. But I kept my mouth shut. Maybe he didn't love her anymore.

No, that was too much to hope for.

So far Patsy and I hadn't come up with a substitute. And we were running out of time.

"I might have a date," Patsy whispered. Daddy didn't hear—or chose not to.

When we kissed Daddy good-night and went upstairs, I asked Patsy, "Who with might you have a date, if I'm not too cu-rious?"

"With whom, you mean," Patsy said in a haughty voice. Without answering the question, she leaned into the mirror and said, "I'm thinking of having cosmetic surgery to change the shape of my face. Make it heart shaped instead of balloon shaped. What do you think?"

I didn't answer her question, either.

"What did Chuck Whipple want when he called the other night?" I said. "He really wanted to talk to me, you know."

Patsy laid a finger alongside each eye and pulled the skin tight. Making herself look exotic.

"I would like to look exotic forever," she said wistfully. "Like Merle Oberon in *Wuthering Heights*."

"Know something?" I don't know why I came unglued right then. Maybe it was the way Patsy changed the subject when I told her Chuck had really wanted to talk to me.

"I'm tired of your selfishness," I yelled. Patsy looked startled. She wasn't used to me yelling.

"How come *you* never comfort *me*?" I went on at the top of my lungs. "I need comforting too, you know. Maybe you should think about that!"

I grabbed a tissue from my pocket and blew my nose noisily.

"It doesn't get any better, you know. The way they said it would. It only gets worse."

I meant Mother. Patsy knew that.

"You're not the only one who misses her," she said. "Besides, I think I miss her more because I'm younger."

That really got me.

"You little creep!" I shouted. "That's the biggest lot of horse manure I ever heard!"

Patsy yelled back, "I wish Mother was here so she could hear the load of crap *you're* dishing out."

I said calmly, "Maybe she is here and she hears every word you're saying and sees everything you're doing."

That stopped her. Suddenly, I felt better. Maybe I should lose my temper with Patsy more often, I thought.

Patsy sighed.

"So. Saturday night. What do we call her, Mrs. Ames or Hey, you?" Patsy squinted at me.

"What's wrong with calling her what we always call her?" I said.

Ten

WHEN I WAS in fifth grade, a girl named Barbara invited me over to her house after school to play. Barbara carried little packets of dry soup mix in her lunch box, into which she dipped slices of apple with the peel still on, and potato chips, and cheese doodles. Her thermos was filled with V8 juice. Plus she wore socks trimmed with lace and all her hair ribbons were color coordinated with her outfits. She wore pink-and-silver harem pants to school one day, and at recess she wouldn't go down the slide for fear the pants would get dirty. Barbara had more outfits than any other person in the class.

Barbara was cool.

Barbara's brother was a genius, she said.

He played the piano before he could walk and he could read the newspaper when he was two. They took him to a special doctor for geniuses, and the doctor said Barbara's brother had an IQ of 200.

"Where's your brother now?" I asked, not knowing what else to say. An IQ of 200 was good. What was my IQ? Probably about seventy-five or eighty. Around there.

"He's at home," Barbara said. "He's finding himself."

"What happens when he finds himself?" I asked, really wanting to know.

Barbara shrugged. "Who knows? In the meantime, my parents are treating him like any other genius kid with an IQ of two hundred. If he wants to eat pizza for breakfast, they let him. If he wants to watch an X-rated movie on cable TV, they say, 'So what harm will it do?' If he wants his girlfriend to sleep over, my mother says, 'At least we know where he is at night.'

"He's sixteen and he should be in college. He already graduated from a special high school for geniuses. If you want to know the truth," Barbara turned and looked straight into my eyes, "he's a mess. I'm glad I'm not a genius."

"Me, too," I said.

When we got to Barbara's house, I tiptoed around, worried I might bump into Barbara's brother. I was both afraid to see him and longing to see him.

Sort of the same way I felt about seeing my mother's ghost.

Ever since I'd said that about Mother hanging around the house, I've been a nervous wreck. I think about ghosts, dream about ghosts, and even though I don't really believe in them, I can't get them out of my mind.

I never did see Barbara's brother that day. I heard music coming from behind his locked door, though. Barbara said he kept his door locked at all times. Her mother left food on a tray outside his room, she said, and when he felt like eating, he unlocked his door and snatched the tray inside. I made several trips to the bathroom while at Barbara's and each trip I checked the floor outside the brother's room, hoping to see an empty plate covered with bones, maybe, but there was nothing.

Mother, I wish you were here, I thought. I need you. There are lots of things I want to say to you. Questions I would like to ask. I knew it wouldn't do any good to wish for these things, but still I did. When we were little, Patsy and I thought if you wished hard enough for something, you'd get it. Sometimes I wish I was young and innocent again.

I would like to discuss the possibility of ghosts with my father, but I know I won't. Baba would be better. She already believes in ghosts. My father is a very practical man, the most practical of men. *He* would definitely not believe. I think it would only make him sad if I suggested Mother was there, in our house, checking out The Tooth's undies.

And if he knew what Patsy and I had *done* with them, he really *would* be pissed.

Eleven

ON MONDAY after school, Chuck Whipple drove up on his three-speed bike.

"Patsy's not here," I told him. "She's at the orthodontist. She'll be back around four-thirty."

"That's okay," Chuck said.

The oven timer beeped loudly, so I told him, "Come on in, if you want. I've got something burning in the oven."

Out of the corner of my eye, I saw Roberta and her mother driving by. A pale face pressed against the car window, a pale hand waved at me.

Chuck followed me out to the kitchen and watched while I took out the cookies, just in time.

"Smells good," he said.

"I always make cookies on Monday," I said. Actually, I make cookies whenever I'm depressed. And sometimes when I'm not. The smell of things baking always cheers me up, makes me think of the days when our house almost always smelled good when Patsy and I got home from school. Our mother timed her baking so stuff would still be warm when we got there.

If I ever have kids, I'm doing the same. Or if I turn out to be a world-famous anything and I have to go around the world on business, my husband will stay home to take care of the kids. I'll tell him he has to learn how to make cakes and cookies and maybe even bread. I think it'd be neat to be married to a man who bakes bread.

"How come you have a three-speed?" I asked Chuck. My cookies today were in the shape of Christmas trees, my favorite. Sometimes I decorated the trees with red and green sprinkles, sometimes I gave them raisins for eyes, the way you do to gingerbread men. Or ladies. And even if trees don't have eyes, so what. They're my cookies. I can do what I want.

"It's an Iowa bike," Chuck said. "We don't have hills out there. It's flat all the way. Nothing but rows and rows of corn."

He seemed to me, at that moment, as exotic a creature as if he'd come straight from Mars. Or California.

I offered him a cookie.

"How come Christmas trees when it's October?" he said.

I shrugged. "I like the trees best. Sometimes I put in raisins for eyes."

He nodded, not finding that odd. "They're very good," he said, taking a bite. "Like Mother used to make."

"This is my mother's recipe," I said. "Only hers were better."

Bright patches of color stained Chuck's cheeks and he said, "I'm sorry."

He had on a blue-and-red plaid shirt, and his cheeks matched the red in his shirt. He grabbed hold of the kitchen doorknob, and I figured he wanted out. I could see he felt terrible about what he'd said. Maybe he felt worse than I did.

"My mother died three years ago," I said, and I heard my voice tremble. No matter how many times I say it, my voice always trembles when I say "My mother died."

"I know and I forgot," he said. "I'm very sorry."

"My father might get married again." I don't know why I said that. I hadn't planned to. "Patsy and I don't want him to. We don't like her. We don't want her for a stepmother. We're going out for dinner with her on Saturday." I almost said "I dread it," but I didn't.

Chuck cleared his throat. "Stepmothers aren't so bad," he said. "I have one. She's pretty nice. I always forget she's not my real mother. I never knew my real mother. She died when I was a baby."

That made me feel really rotten. Now it was my turn to say "I'm sorry."

"I have a whole brother and a half

brother," Chuck went on. "She loves us all the same. There's no difference. She has plenty to go around. Can I have another cookie?"

"Sure. Take all you want. What do you do for fun and games out in Iowa?" I asked him. What Chuck had said seemed to me extraordinary, that his stepmother loved them all the same.

"Well, we have 4H Club meetings," he said. "4H Club is a big deal where I come from."

"What's 4H Club?" I said.

The timer beeped again. I took out the second batch of cookies and they looked better than the first. I set them on a rack to cool and put the last batch in.

"4H Club is about livestock—cows, calves, pigs, lambs," Chuck said. "I got the prize last year for the best pig. She was a beauty. Her tail was perfect. No offense, but her name was Nora."

I looked at him. He wasn't smiling or anything.

"You had a pig named Nora," I said. "How come?"

"I just liked the name," he said. "She took a blue ribbon at the state fair."

I couldn't think of a single thing to say. Oh, your pig named Nora with the perfect tail took a blue ribbon at the state fair. Cool.

"I never knew a person named Nora before I met you," he said. "It must be fate."

We smiled at each other. I didn't know what to say, and I don't think Chuck did either.

The doorbell rang. Yeah!

"My hands are all gooky," I said. "Go see who it is, will you? And if it's the Avon lady, tell her we don't need any."

Chuck went to the door. I heard him talking to someone. He came back and said, "It's a girl named Roberta. She says she has to talk to you about something very important."

"What does she need, an appointment? Roberta! Get out here, you gross-out! We're having a feast!" I shouted.

Roberta was duded up in her new riding skirt her mother ordered from a very exclusive catalog devoted to nothing but expensive riding outfits. Roberta has an anxiety attack if she even gets *near* a horse, but her mother thought the skirt would elongate Roberta, make her look slim. Slimmer.

"I didn't know you had company," said Roberta, lying through her teeth. I figure she saw Chuck at the door as she and her mother drove by, and her mother let her out of the car at the corner and Roberta zoomed home and changed into her elongating riding skirt in record time.

"What's up?" I asked her. "This is Chuck Whipple, Roberta. Chuck, this is Roberta Middleton."

Roberta can be quite aggressive, but usually when she meets a boy for the first time, she becomes positively demure. Casting her eyes down, Roberta whispered "Hi," sort of like a washed-out Scarlett O'Hara, and Chuck said "Hi" back.

"Chuck was just telling me about the 4H Club in Iowa," I said.

The beeper beeped. I took out the last batch of cookies. "Want one?" I asked Roberta.

"Oh, I can't. I'm on a diet," Roberta of the booming voice said so softly I could barely hear her. Behind Chuck's back I bugged out my eyes at her.

"These are special nonfattening cookies," I said.

In a flash, Roberta snatched up a handful.

"Tell Roberta about your pig, Chuck," I said. I don't know why I said that. It was stupid of me.

Chuck choked on a cookie. "Could I have a glass of water, please?" he said.

"You want ice in it?" I asked him.

"No thanks, this is great." Chuck took a long time drinking the water.

"What about your pig?" Roberta said. She is a very curious person, Roberta. She immediately wants to know everything about a person she's just met.

Chuck told her.

Patsy burst in. "I *thought* that was your

bike outside, Chuck," she cried, grabbing a few cookies. *"Qué pasa?"*

"He was just telling us about his pig," Roberta said.

"Chuck has a pig? Well, hey, he can take it to show-and-tell next week. How about it, Chuck?" I thought Patsy was going to slap him on the back. Probably he'd get some crumbs stuck and start choking again, poor guy.

At times Patsy can get a little too hearty. She thought Chuck's pig was a huge joke. She was making fun of his pig because she was nervous. That was before she even found out its name was Nora.

"His pig won first prize at the 4H Club fair," Roberta went on, liking it that she knew things about Chuck Patsy didn't know. "And guess what the pig's name was?"

"Hey." Patsy ate a few trees. "Like your new skirt, kid. It makes you look positively emaciated. What was your pig's name, Chuck?"

"Nora," Chuck said, probably wondering how he could get out of this joint in one piece.

Patsy's hand paused in midair over the cookie plate.

"How come?" she said.

"I liked the name," Chuck said, shrugging. "I think it's pretty. And she was a pretty pig, so that's what I called her." He didn't say anything about her tail, for which I was grateful.

"I didn't know there was such a thing as a pretty pig," Patsy said. I could see she was jealous—she never had a pig named after *her*.

Changing the subject with a clang, Patsy said, "I've just had the worst afternoon of my life. He reset my retainer, and now my teeth feel as if they're nestled up inside my nose. And I have to go back next week so he can reset it again."

"Well, I have to go now," Chuck said quickly. "Thanks for the cookies."

When he'd ridden away, Roberta said,

"He has very sexy eyes. I didn't know boys from Iowa had sexy eyes."

"I bet he was disappointed I wasn't here when he got here," Patsy said. "Wasn't he?"

"No," I said, thinking before I spoke. "I don't believe he was. Roberta, did Chuck seem disappointed Patsy wasn't here?"

"Heck, no," Roberta said. "Too many folks at the orgy is never a good idea. Right, Nora?"

Right.

Twelve

MEN ARE like streetcars, Baba says. Miss one, you can catch the next one that comes along.

True or false, I myself think this is a sexist remark.

Baba says there was no such thing as a sexist remark when she was a girl.

When Baba was young, it was wartime. World War II, not the Civil War, she adds with a wry smile.

"We were all in love in those days," Baba told us. "All the beautiful young men were in uniform, so brave, so patriotic, going off to God knows what. To defend their country. It was hard not to fall in love, I can tell you. And, I hasten to add," Baba said, making owl eyes at us over the top of her glasses, "we were chaste. We did not fall into the hay with every Tom, Dick, and Harry. I think I can say, in all honesty and relatively speaking, we were, by today's standards, chaste."

Wide-eyed, Patsy said, "What does 'chaste' mean?" Patsy liked to put Baba on the spot. Baba was not of the generation that called a spade a spade, sexwise.

Baba blushed and gave a little laugh and plunged in.

" 'Chaste' means you treat your body with respect, which it deserves," Baba said. "You only have one body. It is yours and no one else's. You are the boss of that body. You control it completely. You do not let strangers take license with your body. It is very precious and should be treated as such."

Baba paused. How to proceed. What more to say to a rapt audience?

"Does that explain what 'chaste' means, girls? Do I make myself perfectly clear?"

"Sure," I said. I was embarrassed. I thought Baba had done a pretty good job and that Patsy should let her off the hook.

But Patsy was not as easily satisfied as I was.

Innocent as any two-year-old, Patsy said, "What does 'fall into the hay' mean, Baba?"

"Give me a break, Patsy," Baba said, losing patience. "It means 'get into bed,' as you know perfectly well."

Baba got to her feet. "I really must run," she said. "I have a dinner engagement with an old beau."

Baba had a lot of old beaus. She'd been engaged six times, she told us. "I had trouble making up my mind," she said.

"Can I ask you one more question?" Patsy asked.

"All right, one," Baba said.

"Were you chaste when you married Grandfather?"

I gasped. Patsy had gone too far. Patsy frequently goes too far, however far "too far" is.

Baba studied her image in the hall mirror. She bit her lips and pinched her cheeks to make them rosy.

"That's impertinent, Patsy," she said. "And really doesn't deserve an answer. One rudeness, however, is no excuse for another. My answer is: Need you ask? Your mother would say the same if she were here. Listen to me because I know what I'm talking about."

"You are too fresh, Patsy," I said when Baba went to powder her nose. "She's our grandmother, after all."

"At least she didn't say 'Your body is your temple,'" Patsy said. "That's what some kids' grandmothers tell them. A temple!" Patsy hooted. "How does that grab you?"

"Just wait," I said. "I can see you giving your daughter the straight skinny when she asks you about sex. You'll hem and haw, and when you're finished the poor little tyke won't know squat about the subject. You'll probably send her screaming from the room and she'll have bad dreams for about a month."

"As I think I have said, I do not plan to have a daughter, or any other kind of child," Patsy said firmly. "But if I do, I'll give it to her straight. No beating around the bush. I will simply tell her the facts of life, as I see them."

"Ah, that's the key," I said. "As *you* see them. You are warped, not to mention uninformed. You are also off the wall."

"Buzz off," Patsy said.

"I bet Chuck knows all about sex," she said, shooting me a sly glance, "being a country boy and all, and a member of the 4H Club. There's probably nothing he doesn't know. The 4H Club is loaded with animals, and animals have very active sex lives."

"So do plants, jerk," I said. I didn't want to talk about sex. I had better things to think about.

"And insects," Baba threw in, returning from powdering her nose. "And fish. I do believe, my dears, that sex is here to stay."

"For a grandmother, Baba," Patsy said, "you're pretty racy."

"This is fine talk," Baba said. She had come to our house for Tuesday dinner. She comes to our house for dinner a lot. Baba has many talents, but cooking isn't one of them. Patsy and I stuck an onion in the chicken and shoved it into a 350-degree oven. Nothing to it. Baba mashed the potatoes. Her potatoes have lots of lumps. She says she likes them with lumps.

Daddy bought an apple pie for dessert.

Our date with The Tooth is on, Daddy told us. For Saturday. We would all go in a merry little band to the dinner theater and have dinner and watch the show.

"Mrs. Ames said to tell you girls nothing would give her greater pleasure than to spend an evening getting to know you both," Daddy told us.

Patsy excused herself. "I have to go burn off my bad karma," she said.

After I went to bed I couldn't sleep.

There was too much else going on. I wondered why Patsy and I couldn't find someone to blast The Tooth out of Daddy's mind. Someone he would love and so would we. There must be plenty of people who'd *love* to marry Daddy. He is a very excellent and outstanding man.

Friday night we were going to Dee's wine and cheese reception, and Saturday we were all tied up with The Tooth and Daddy.

Life in the fast lane.

Maybe we could find the girl of Daddy's dreams at Dee's wine and cheese thing. I doubt it, though.

Thirteen

"WHO'S THE BABE in the hat?" I heard a man say. He had a droopy mustache and deep grooves on either side of his mouth. He meant Baba.

Her new hat, which she'd bought just for the wine and cheese one-man show, was eye-catching. It was black, with a flat crown and a wide brim. Getting into the artsy-craftsy spirit of the evening, Baba also wore her black cape with a red lining and her tall black boots.

"If only you had a mask, you'd look like Zorro," Patsy had said as we piled into Daddy's car, bald tires and all.

"Zorro who?" Baba said.

"You know. *The Mark of Zorro.* We saw it last week on TV," I said.

"I always say a hat puts the finishing touch on a costume," Baba said. "I'm so glad hats are back."

"I didn't know they'd been away," Daddy said. "We'd better get a move on. I've noticed that people who go to art galleries for a one-man show tend to be very big eaters. They gobble up everything in sight. I think it's because most of them haven't had a square meal in a week. So if we want some wine and cheese, we'd best move fast."

When we got there, sure enough, everyone was eating and drinking. No one was paying any attention to the paintings, the artwork. There were long lines at the refreshment tables. Mother's portrait had the place of honor. Some people wandered over to it with their drinks and studied it intently, tilting their heads from side to side, squinching up their faces.

"Who is that woman?" Patsy said in a loud voice, to no one in particular.

A woman with a baby strapped to her back turned and said, "She's a mystery woman. Isn't she wonderful?"

A man with a baby strapped to *his* back came over, and he and the woman discussed whether or not the woman should nurse the baby here or in the ladies' room.

"I don't think this is a nursing type crowd," the man said, looking around critically. "It looks pretty suburban to me."

Both babies roused themselves as if on signal, raised their little heads, and started bawling.

"Mention food and those kids go crazy," the man said proudly.

"Are they twins?" I asked the man.

"Not that I know of," the man said.

A man wearing a hairy cowboy hat and hairy sideburns and high-heeled cowboy boots slid into the space left when the man and woman went off with the babies.

"Would that go with my draperies or would it clash?" He meant our mother's portrait. "I have absolutely no eye for color." The man turned to me. "My furniture is upholstered in a beige fabric, sort of nubby, and my draperies are red and green and beige. What do you think?"

"It's not for sale," Patsy said.

The man's eyes snapped open and looked as if they might explode. "What do you *mean,* not for sale? I never heard of such a thing! They got me all the way out here and then tell me it's not for sale? That's practically fraudulent. I have never been so insulted in my entire life."

Patsy and I watched him stomp off on the high-heeled cowboy boots.

"My horse, my horse, my kingdom for a horse," I said.

"Those heels take a lot of practice," Patsy said. "That dude'll be lucky to make it down the steps. You know," Patsy said, smiling, "I think I like these wine and cheese affairs. There are more weirdos at them than you usually see at parties. I think I'll have a glass of wine. How about you?"

"You better not," I said. "Daddy will

scalp you if he finds out you're drinking wine."

"There she is." A pretty woman smiled at Mother in her red shawl. "That's Buffy, all right. Dee told me she was here. It's a glorious likeness. We were friends when we were children."

That's what they called our mother, "Buffy." Her real name was Elizabeth.

"She's our mother," Patsy said.

"Of course. Of course. How absolutely perfect that I should run into you." The woman put out her hands and each of us took one.

"My name is Jane Morris. Your mother was like a sister to me when we were children. We lived on the same street, went to the same school. Then my family moved to the West Coast and we lost touch. Is your father here? I'd like to tell him how sorry I was when I heard your mother had died. Dee wrote me, but I was out of the country and didn't get the letter for ages."

"I think he's over there," Patsy said,

standing on tiptoes, scanning the crowd. "Nora, go see if you can find Daddy, tell him a friend of Mother's is here."

"You go," I said. "I'll stay here and keep her company. You're much better at finding people than I am."

I talked to Jane Morris while Patsy went for Daddy. She told me she had her own public relations firm in Chicago and was in New York on business. Dee had sent her an invitation, never thinking she'd come out from the city for this party.

"I had to come," Jane Morris said. "Something made me come." She told me all sorts of things about our mother I'd never heard before. About how they used to play baseball in the schoolyard every day after lunch. "Your mother was a terrific second baseman," she said. "And you should've seen her when we started to go to boy-girl parties. That was in fifth grade, I think, maybe sixth. We played Spin the Bottle. Oh, how she spun that bottle." Jane Morris rolled her eyes. "It was a sight to see! No boy in the place was safe. She'd just grab hold of whoever the bottle pointed to and kiss him until she was ready to let go. She was very strong. The boys didn't have a chance. I used to watch in awe and admiration. I was kind of a goofy kid, young for my age. But your mother was a ringleader. And when we went to dancing school, all done up in our velvet dresses and white gloves, Buffy'd dash across the floor and nab the boy she wanted to dance with."

Oh, I could just see her, racing to be the first to reach a certain boy. Her long legs flashing as she skidded across the dance floor. How I wish I'd been there. She'd have that determined look on her face that I remembered, too. And she'd have on her black velvet dress and her Mary Jane shoes and little white socks. We have a picture of her in that outfit. She told Patsy and me that when she was eleven or twelve all girls wore little white socks and didn't get to wear silk stockings until they went to college. She said panty hose hadn't been invented when she was a girl. Patsy and I didn't believe her. Mother had a tendency to exaggerate to make a story better.

Someone laughed close by and I thought, *She's here!* But when I turned to look, I saw a blond woman waving her hands and tossing her hair out of her eyes in a girlish way, although she was no girl. And her laugh wasn't the least like Mother's.

When I was in second grade, I had a friend named Stephanie. She and her sister Lu had an imaginary friend named Calvin. They took Calvin everywhere, on picnics and to climb trees and into the woods to hunt wildflowers. I thought it was kind of strange they both had the same imaginary friend, but I didn't say anything. They even set a place for Calvin at their family's dinner table. Stephanie and Lu had three brothers and two sisters, so when Calvin (who was a picky eater anyway) sat down at the table, nobody even noticed he was there.

Could I be imagining my mother's ghost?

Fourteen

Next morning Patsy floated in with my breakfast on a tray. I hate breakfast in bed. Patsy thinks it's classy.

"It's Martha Stewart here!" she cried.

Martha Stewart's this perfect person who writes books telling how to throw a wedding reception for three hundred and fifty guests and do all the work yourself. She came to our local bookstore to autograph her books, and there was a line that reached all around the block.

"First you bone a hundred turkeys," she starts off. Then she rushes on to the cake. "Separate twelve dozen eggs, making sure no whites get into the yolks." Or vice versa. I'm never sure which shouldn't get into which.

"Sit up, Norrie! Don't forget breakfast's the most important meal of the day!" Patsy cried.

I snuggled deeper into my pillow and made noises.

"Sit up, I said! I went to all this trouble just for you. We have here eggs Benedict with hollandaise sauce, freshly squeezed orange juice, pits and all, and cinnamon nut coffee cake," Patsy read off a menu.

I sat up. Sometimes it's easier to give in than to fight her. Besides, it all sounded very delicious.

Patsy slapped the tray down on my stomach. "Enjoy! *Bon appétit!*"

"You are a fraud," I said sourly. The string of the tea bag dangled limply over the side of the cup and the toast sat in the toast rack getting colder by the minute. A sad little dab of marmalade completed the scene.

Patsy and I bought that toast rack at a flea market. "It's very British," the flea market lady told us. "They always put toast in one of those gizmos."

"How come?" I said. "It'll only get cold faster."

"They *like* cold toast," the lady said. "You can have it for a buck. I'm losing money on the deal, but I have to wind up here and get to Florida."

"All we've got is fifty cents," Patsy said.

"It's yours." The lady handed over the toast rack and we were stuck with it. . . .

"Okay." Patsy plunked down on the foot of my bed. I could tell she wanted to be friends and forget Chuck.

Daddy knocked and stuck his head in.

"Just wanted to make sure we're on for tonight," he said. "I'm about to call Wynne Ames and set a time. Seven all right for you? Wear something pretty. Dresses, please. This is an event. I want you both to look smashing."

The Tooth is "in fashion"—a fashion consultant or something unreal like that. I can take fashion or leave it alone.

"That Mrs. Morris is very nice, Daddy," Patsy said. "She told Nora lots of interesting things about Mother when she was little. Maybe you should ask her for a date."

"Sure," Daddy said, "fine." And he disappeared.

"I don't think Mrs. Morris's divorced," Patsy said. "She didn't *look* divorced."

"Give it up," I told her. "And get off my bed. If I'm going to eat this mess, I want peace and quiet, not some great lump bouncing on the mattress."

That was a mistake. Patsy started bouncing up and down vigorously, and the tea slopped over the cold toast and hit the marmalade.

"I don't have a dress," Patsy said. "I'm wearing my fake leather mini and my denim shirt. If The Tooth doesn't like it, tough."

"You wear that and you might have to stay home," I said. "Daddy'd have a fit, never mind The Tooth."

"Yeah." Patsy grinned her evil grin. "I might have to stay home and brood all night about you guys having a good time in Darien." I listened to her cackling like the wicked witch of the West all the way downstairs.

You know how sometimes you think something's going to be absolutely awful? Like a school dance in the gym. Or a party someone asks you to and you don't know a soul except the person who asked you, but you go anyway because you talk yourself into going? Mostly, when you expect the worst, things turn out to be not as bad as expected. Well, our dinner with Daddy and The Tooth turned out to be so much worse than I thought it would be it wasn't even funny. By the end of the evening I wanted to slide under the table and disappear.

In the first place, Chuck Whipple was at the dinner theater with his family. Sitting three tables away from us. I had just sat down when I saw Chuck. He saw me and waved a little.

Patsy had cleaned up her act and looked pretty nice in her navy blue dress, which is way too tight across her bust. I looked sort of cute in my red-and-white striped dress, which resembles a beach umbrella. It is also pretty long, halfway to my ankles, which was just as well because I could feel the big rip in my panty hose getting bigger and bigger as I ate my soup. Every time I breathed, that rip expanded, up and down my leg. Probably by the time I got up the whole leg would be dragging on the floor as it followed me like a puppy all the way to the ladies' room.

"Such a pretty frock," The Tooth purred, checking me out. She does that, sort of purrs when she's being insincere, which is most of the time. She takes inventory of you with her eyes, checks out every wrinkle, every spot of mustard, sees every safety pin holding your underwear together. She herself, as we already knew, bought Victoria's Secret stuff up the wazoo.

"She looks at me as if she thinks I have hairy armpits," Patsy had said after her first experience with The Tooth's X-ray vision.

"But you *do* have hairy armpits," I had reminded her. Patsy doesn't shave under her arms or eat red meat. If there's a connection there, it escapes me.

Now, to set matters straight, I said, "It's not a frock, it's a dress."

The Tooth looked at me oddly, then said to my father, "Perhaps we should have some champagne, Sam." She laid her hand on Daddy's arm. "In celebration of this momentous event, being with your family tonight. I'm thrilled to be a part of it."

Daddy called the waiter over and ordered champagne. "Two glasses, please," he said. That meant none for us. I have never had champagne. Patsy sneaked some last year at our cousin's wedding. It made her tipsy, as well as sick as a dog. Patsy says she may never drink champagne again.

The waiter brought two champagne glasses and two plain glasses for Patsy and me.

"Are we having Shirley Temples?" Patsy asked, wide-eyed. I kicked her under the table. We were at the awkward age when we were too old for Shirley Temples and too young for champagne.

We drank Perrier with a twist of lemon.

I managed to sit so I could keep Chuck Whipple under scrutiny. He kept looking over at us. Too bad there was no dancing here. Maybe he'd ask me to dance.

The Tooth kept putting her hand on Daddy's arm. Oh ho, I thought. It's the old territorial imperative routine. A dog pees on a tree, the next dog who comes along pees on the same tree, only *higher up*. That's territorial imperative. So I put my hand on Daddy's arm, a little higher than where The Tooth's hand rested, sending her a message she could not fail to understand.

Speaking of peeing, during the lull between dessert and the beginning of the play, I excused myself to go to the ladies' room. Never miss an opportunity to pee, as the Duke of Wellington once said. Patsy was gabbing to Daddy about something so I went without her.

When I came out of the ladies', I

bumped smack into Chuck Whipple. He acted surprised to see me, even though we'd been tossing goo-goo eyes at each other all evening.

"Come on over and meet my parents," Chuck said.

"Sure, that'd be fine," I said. I followed him to the table. Chuck's father stood up and shook my hand. His brother did, too. The girlfriend hardly acknowledged my presence. Chuck's stepmother was friendly and nice.

Without warning, Chuck's stepmother got up and said, "Nora, come along with me, dear," and she sort of pushed me in front of her, all the way to the ladies' room.

"But I was just there," I said. "I don't . . ."

Chuck's stepmother reached behind me and tugged at my dress. I backed off. "What's the matter?" I said.

"Your dress got tucked up inside your panty hose," she said. "I just pulled it down. Now everything's fine. I got you in quick before anyone saw. There now. Turn so I can make sure it's right."

Face aflame, I did as she said. My dress had been hiked up high, tucked inside the waistband of my panty hose, showing my bare behind, not to mention my panty hose full of holes, hanging out there for the world to see.

"I'm sure no one saw, Nora," Chuck's stepmother said. "Rest easy."

I could die. The rest of the evening was ruined. I tried to act as if I was enjoying the play, but I was in the pits. He had seen my rear end hanging out, my panty hose that looked like Swiss cheese. He must've had a good laugh. Oh, I could just die, go right through the floor and not come back up for fifty years.

I never wanted to see Chuck Whipple ever again. Never, ever again.

Fifteen

When we first got home I dry-heaved into the toilet bowl for a while. Patsy kept asking me what was wrong. I couldn't talk to her, couldn't tell her what had happened. I couldn't speak of the unspeakable.

I couldn't sleep. I kept seeing myself walking across the restaurant with my bare behind hanging out. No wonder they smiled as I passed by. No wonder they all laughed and pointed at me. Chuck Whipple must've been sorry he asked me over to his table to meet his parents. They must've thought I was some total weirdo, some cretin who didn't know enough to pull her skirt down. Nerd. Oaf. There weren't enough words to describe me. I was a loser.

At last, after tossing and turning like a whirligig, I went down to get something to eat.

It was dark downstairs, but I didn't need any light. I went to the refrigerator and got an orange, which I took into the living room to eat. I brought along a paper napkin to catch the drips. Still in the dark, I sat on the couch and ate the orange. It tasted good. I like the dark. I like sitting by myself and thinking about things. Life. Mother. Death. Bare skin hanging out of holey panty hose. I kept seeing Chuck Whipple with his mouth open, laughing at me. Making fun of me. If Mother were here she'd know what to say to make me feel better.

It took me a few seconds to realize I wasn't alone.

The sound of a man clearing his throat made me jump.

"Daddy? It's me, Nora."

He didn't answer, but I could hear him breathing.

"What's wrong, Daddy?"

"I thought the evening went well," he said.

Not for me, I thought.

"I'm sorry you don't like Wynne. She thinks both you and Patsy are charmers." His voice was only a little blurred, a little angry.

"I think you could've pretended you liked her," he said.

"I'm sorry," I said, unable to say more.

My father raised his voice and in his formal way, he said, "Your mother would understand. She'd know right now I'm just going through the motions, connecting the dots, so to speak. If she were here, she'd give me her blessing." He paused. "Of course, if she were here, it wouldn't be necessary, would it?"

His voice sounded very tired.

The down cushions on the couch sighed as they always did when someone sat on them. Across from me I could see the vague outline of my father sitting in his usual big chair.

I tried to turn, to see who was there, but my head wouldn't move. I thought I might be hallucinating. I put out my hand and felt my fingers held, a warm touch. A touch so warm, so loving, so familiar I was not afraid. Then I felt cold run up my arm. It was a terrible cold, unlike any cold I had ever known before.

I must've made a noise. My father said, "What's wrong, darling?"

I wasn't sure if he was talking to me or to her.

It didn't matter. She was there, in the room. I knew she was. We sat in silence, the three of us. I wished I had a sweater. The cold was like a presence. I scarcely dared swallow for fear of disturbing the quiet.

She will give us a sign and soon. Very soon, I thought.

Gradually the cold receded. So gradually it took me a while to realize it was gone. She had gone, too. I longed to turn on the light, to see if there was any trace of her, to see my father's face. I wondered if he knew.

"Well." My father's voice sounded thin and very far away. "I'm going to turn in. Good night, darling." I listened to him climb the stairs slowly, heard him go into his room and close the door.

I got up stiffly, feeling old before my time. Still in the dark, I went to Patsy's room and laid my hand against her face.

Patsy sat up.

"Your hand's freezing," she said crossly.

I opened my mouth to say, Mother came back. She was here.

Instead, I said, "What's the other reason Daddy wants to marry her?"

"It's the middle of the night, Nora. You must be on drugs," Patsy said.

"I want to know," I said.

"I told you. He's a gentleman of the old school. He's lonely. She's got him painted into a corner. She expects him to marry her. I could've told you that. Now scram."

Patsy lay down and promptly began to snore.

There were other questions I wanted to

ask. They could wait. I wanted to think about what had happened, go over it in my head. To be absolutely sure.

I got into bed. Pictures played against my eyelids. Only happy ones, no terrible ones of me and my bare behind. We were all together—Mother, Daddy, Patsy, and me. All moving in slow motion and smiling.

I got out of bed and went downstairs again. I turned on the light in the living room. The cushion, the one that had sighed, bore a faint imprint. Of what I did not know. I thought about plumping it up to make it fat and smooth, the way Mother likes them. Then I pulled my hand back. I decided to leave it alone, the way it was.

At the foot of the stairs, I paused. I felt a slight pressure on my arm. And when I turned, which I did reluctantly, and because there was no way in the world that I could not have turned, my heart thudded wildly in my throat.

And there was absolutely no one there.

Sixteen

THAT WAS on Saturday. All of that happened on a Saturday.

Next morning I woke up on the wrong side of the bed. My head hurt and my mouth felt furry and I felt as if I was still blushing from last night. A dull ache in my stomach didn't help. Lucky for Patsy she didn't show up with breakfast on a tray for me again. I probably would've thrown it at her.

After I took a shower and washed my hair, I felt much better. And when I remembered the way the couch cushions had sighed last night, I was so excited and thrilled that the panty hose business seemed to fade away. Almost.

First I wanted to see Baba. There were

plenty of things I had to ask her. I planned to tell her about Mother coming back to the house last night. It crossed my mind that, although Baba believed in ghosts per se, she might not believe me when I told her about our mother. She might think I was going cuckoo. I wanted her to listen to me, to understand and to explain, if possible, exactly what had happened. I knew Baba would have some of the answers. Not all. I didn't expect her to have all. Nobody has that many.

I dialed Baba's number. It rang and rang. Maybe she was in the tub. Baba was into long, relaxing hot baths. She poured so much stuff into her tub it was a wonder there was room for her. Bath salts, bath oils, some special powder she bought that was supposed to ease aches and pains.

"Not that I'm old, you understand," she'd said. "I'm more middle-aged. Middle age goes on until you're about eighty. Then you slide on into senility. I do not plan on ever being senile. Come to think of it, I don't know a whole lot of people who do! However, I will do all I can to remain alert, bright eyed, and indefatigable."

Knowing Baba was good for my vocabulary. She was always telling Patsy and me to look it up. Sometimes we did, sometimes we didn't.

I was about to hang up when Baba answered. Her voice sounded sort of wobbly and strange.

"I won't be going to church with you this morning, I'm afraid," she said. "I'm not well, not well at all."

Baba wards off germs with vitamins. She does aerobics and yoga. Once she had the flu, but that's because the flu nails everyone, young and old—it doesn't care who you are.

"What's wrong?" I said.

"Well, I did the stupidest thing," Baba said. "I tripped and fell over that little rag rug I have in the bathroom. I did something to my wrist. I think it's probably just sprained, not broken. It hurts, though. And it's swollen. I'll wait until tomorrow and if it still bothers me, I'll go to the doctor."

"Are you hurt?" I said. "I'll get Daddy."

"No, don't. I'll be all right, Nora. I'll rest today. I've got the papers. They'll keep me busy."

"What's the trouble?" Daddy said. He'd been listening to my end of the conversation.

"Baba tripped on her little rag rug and did something to her wrist," I said. "She sounds kind of shook up."

"Tell her I'm on my way," Daddy said, patting his pockets for his keys. He always does that. "Tell her to sit tight and I'll be right there."

"Can I come?" I said.

"If you're ready to go now," Daddy said. "This minute."

I left a note for Patsy telling her we'd gone to Baba's. She was in the shower washing her hair, and that usually took her about half an hour.

Baba opened her door as far as the chain lock would allow. She peered out at Daddy and me. Her hair was a mess and she wore the blush-colored robe with her initials on the sleeve we'd given her for her birthday.

It occurred to me I'd never seen her with her hair a mess before. She was usually very careful about her appearance. It made her look younger, somehow.

"Would you like some coffee, Sam?" she asked when she let us in.

"Sit down, darling. I'll get it," Daddy said. He poured two cups, one for Baba and one for him. He knows I hate coffee.

"Let's see that wrist," Daddy said.

Reluctantly, Baba held it out for his inspection. "It's only a sprain," she said. "I can manage fine. It'll go down in a few days. It's nothing."

"Looks like something to me," Daddy said. "I think we better go to the emergency room and have it X-rayed."

Baba pulled a face and said, "Don't make a fuss, Sam. You know how I feel about you making a fuss."

Daddy insisted and I helped Baba get dressed and we went to the emergency room. Fortunately it wasn't crowded, so they took Baba right away. X-rays showed she'd broken a small bone in her right wrist. A nice young doctor said Baba would have to have a cast. "Only a little cast," the doctor said, smiling at us. I caught Daddy smiling back. She'd make a very nice stepmother, I thought. A little young for Daddy, but who cares? It'd be cool to have a doctor for a stepmother.

"Oh, for heaven's sake," Baba said. "What a to-do! I knew I never should've bought that little rug. This is ridiculous."

"Do you live alone?" the doctor asked Baba.

"I certainly do," Baba said. It was a point of pride with her.

"She'll come back with us until she's better," Daddy announced. "We'll look after her."

"I can look after myself," Baba said. She's very stubborn at times.

After she had her cast put on, we went to her condo to pick up some of her things and drove her home with us.

I was glad, and I think Baba was, too, although she wouldn't admit it. I liked the idea of taking care of her. And it would give me a chance to tell her about Mother and hear what she had to say.

Seventeen

"OH, COOL," Patsy said when she saw Baba's cast. "We'll get all our friends to autograph it."

"Spare me," Baba said. "Give me a break, Patsy."

"You got one—you want another?" Patsy said.

Baba moved into our guest room. The visiting nurse service said it would send someone over a few times a week to give Baba a bath, fix her hair, tie her shoes if necessary.

"I'm not having a perfect stranger give me a bath," Baba said. "I am not an invalid, am I?"

"Well, yes," we said. "You are." Daddy

went out and bought Baba an armload of romance novels—Barbara Cartland, Danielle Steele. Barbara Cartland is this ancient person who talks her stories into a machine and has gotten very rich doing so. She is British and related to the royal family and wears nothing but pink.

When I told Roberta about Barbara Cartland, she accused me of making it all up. Would that my imagination were that fertile. I'd talk a few stories into a machine, too, and also make big bucks doing so.

I still had not told Patsy about our mother returning and sitting on the couch and taking my hand in hers. I still had not thought it through. Too much had happened.

The doctor gave Baba some medicine to help her sleep. Her wrist hurt. "If you want anything in the night," I told her, "just holler." Maybe I could get Baba alone that way. It'd be just her and me at 3:00 A.M., and then I'd tell her about the astonishing event and get her opinion.

Monday morning Patsy and I got up

early to fix Baba breakfast and make her comfortable. Daddy was going to his office late. We would all work together to take care of her.

"I have to go to the orthodontist's after school," Patsy said. "But I'll come straight home from there. I can read you the newspaper, Baba. I will massage your back so you don't get bedsores. You can dictate your thank-you letters to me, Baba. For all the candy and flowers and stuff your friends will send you."

"Patsy, you are a dear, good child," Baba said, "but I am not helpless." Patsy really liked getting into stuff. Having Baba in our home with a broken wrist made Patsy feel sort of like Florence Nightingale, I guess.

Daddy fixed a little table on the left side of Baba's bed and put the telephone on it, along with a box of tissues and Baba's medicine and some water. Baba's friend Bernice would come at lunchtime with something delicious for both of them to eat.

When I got home from school, the house

was quiet. I went into Baba's room. She had fallen asleep sitting up with her glasses on. The radio was playing a golden oldie. I took off her glasses carefully so as not to wake her, and she slipped down under the covers without a ripple.

The kitchen was spotless, which always made me nervous. I decided to bake some cookies to louse up the kitchen and cheer myself up. How come I always seem to need cheering up on Mondays? I asked myself. Last Monday, when Chuck Whipple came over, and now this Monday.

And no one was coming over.

I took out the sugar and the flour and set them on the kitchen counter. They looked kind of dopey and expectant, sitting there, waiting for my magic touch. I went into the living room and sat down on the couch that sighed.

You're losing it, kid, I told myself. I carry on quite a fascinating dialogue with myself at times.

A sudden noise at the back door made me jump.

It was Chuck Whipple, still oozing sex appeal all over the doormat, which said GO AWAY in big letters. (My uncle Joe had given that mat to my father last Christmas. They both thought it was very funny. I could take it or leave it.)

My first impulse was to hide. Pretend I wasn't there. But I wanted to test him, see if he showed any signs he'd seen me with my big fat butt hanging out last Saturday night. Maybe he'd tease me about it. I got red just thinking about what I'd do if he mentioned it.

"Oh, hi," I said. I made myself look right at him.

He wasn't going to say anything. Even if he'd seen what happened, he wouldn't let on. He was too polite.

And he was here, in our kitchen. He must still like me!

I had to laugh. And maybe shout, I was so glad to see Chuck. "Hi," I said again.

"I thought you always baked cookies on Monday," Chuck said. I guess he hadn't seen me and my butt. I almost fainted with relief. I'd never noticed that his smile was tipsy, one-sided. Or that he had a dimple on the side he smiled on. How come I'd never noticed that before? It was a very important thing.

"My grandmother's asleep," I told him. "She broke her wrist, so she's staying with us until she gets better."

"I'm sorry," Chuck said. "I'm really sorry." In a rush, not looking at me, he said, "I'm trying out for the basketball team tomorrow. My mother and father said I should. I probably won't make it."

"Oh, I hope you do," I said.

"They think I should make more friends," Chuck said. "They think if I'm on the basketball team, I'll make friends. But I don't know." He stared at me and I felt my cheeks burning. "So far, you're my only friend. Well, you and Patsy."

"Patsy's not here," I said. "She's at the orthodontist."

"You always say that," Chuck said. "She must spend a lot of time there. Is the orthodontist a really good-looking guy or something?"

"Not so's you'd notice," I said.

"Have you ever moved?"

It was the thing he'd really wanted to talk about all along. I knew that without knowing how I knew.

"No," I said. "I've always lived here, in this town. It must be tough, moving to a strange place, getting used to everything all over. Like school and kids and teachers. A new house. I imagine it's hard for you."

I had said the right things. I could see the gloom lift off him and sail into the atmosphere, a great gray balloon that would not be missed.

"Oh, I can handle it," he said. "It's nothing I can't handle. Not too much of a hassle. It's just that sometimes I don't know where I'm going or how I'm going to get there. You know?"

I did, sort of.

A sudden thought erupted in my head. I would like him to kiss me, I thought. I would like him to *try* to kiss me. I am almost fourteen years old and a boy has never tried to kiss me. When my mother was my age, she had already kissed plenty of boys playing Spin the Bottle. Jane Morris said my mother just grabbed hold of those boys and kissed 'em until she felt like letting go. I would like to do that. I wondered what Chuck Whipple would do if all of a sudden I grabbed him and started kissing him.

Somebody had to make the first move. I walked slowly toward Chuck, who was standing by the kitchen door. I had almost reached him. My head was up and I kept my eyes on his.

"Hey, you guys!" Patsy shouted. "What is this, some kind of a tryst or something?"

Patsy had a way of clearing the room, all right. Chuck got out of there, fast. Thanks, Patsy.

"Well." Patsy crossed her arms on her chest and glared at me. "If it wasn't a tryst, what was it? It sure looked like a tryst to me."

"I don't even know what a tryst is," I said. "Where do you get these words anyway?"

"From one of those papers at the supermarket checkout," Patsy said. "They're always talking 'trysts,' so I figured it had something to do with sex. I looked it up. It means a secret meeting between lovers. So I thought Chuck Whipple might be putting the moves on you due to a tryst."

"Oh, get real," I said. What would she do if I told her I was thinking of putting the moves on Chuck Whipple?

Eighteen

ON TUESDAY Dee Dulin came to see Baba, carrying a bunch of daisies dotted with little blue flowers, as well as a packet of paper cocktail napkins that said, Age Is Only Important if You're a Cheese.

"My sentiments exactly," Baba said. She made me stick one of the napkins on the refrigerator door with a magnet, where it could be seen and appreciated by all.

"You look marvelous," Dee told Baba. "No need to ask how you're getting on."

"Well, Sam and the girls are treating me like royalty," Baba said. "I may stay here forever," she joked.

Lots of people sent flowers. Baba got a

card and bouquet of freesias and anenomes from The Tooth. The note read, "Best love and wishes for a speedy recovery."

"She's moving in for the kill," I heard Baba murmur. "It was sweet of her to send them. I'm not looking a gift horse in the mouth, girls."

"Not with those teeth," Patsy said. Which wasn't at all kind but sent us into a fit of giggles.

The telephone rang as Patsy and I were getting Baba's supper ready. Roberta's mother had sent over some of her world-famous meat loaf and a mushroom casserole that looked like dog barf, which we were heating up for Baba. Daddy was working late.

"Hello there, Patsy!" The Tooth's voice rang out as I answered.

"I'm Nora," I said.

"Oh, you two girls sound so much alike," she said, as practically everyone did. "Is your father there?"

"No, he's working," I said.

"Would you give him a message, please? Tell him I have to go to San Francisco unexpectedly tomorrow and then on to Hong Kong, so our trip will have to be postponed. Will you tell him that for me, please? He'll understand."

"Sure," I said, leaping for joy. Maybe this meant the romance was over.

"The Tooth called and said she had to go to Frisco and on to Hong Kong, so her and Daddy's trip will have to be postponed," I told Baba, grinning. Patsy was busily autographing Baba's cast against Baba's wishes.

"Good Luck to You and the Boston Celtics," Patsy wrote with a Magic Marker on Baba's cast.

"Now really, Patsy," Baba said. "Such nonsense." She had just lifted her fork, laden with Roberta's mother's meat loaf, to her mouth when the phone rang again.

"It's Roberta," Patsy said. "Ten bucks says it's Roberta."

"Hello," I said.

It was Roberta. Lucky for me I'm not a betting woman.

"Is that meat loaf delicious or what?" Roberta said. "Want me to tell you what's in it?"

"No, let me guess," I said.

"Oatmeal," Roberta trumpeted. "And sauerkraut. You can't even tell it's sauerkraut, though."

"I'm not telling Baba," I said. "I'm letting her guess."

"How about a game of strippola poker Saturday night?" Roberta said. "My parents are going to a black-tie affair. They'll be late."

"Gosh, I don't think we can, Roberta," I said. Patsy let her jaw drop, revealing a mouthful of Roberta's mother's mushroom casserole.

"Patsy and me might have a date," I said ungrammatically.

A dense silence gripped Roberta's end of the line.

"You mean to tell me your father'd let

you go out? With a boy? We're talking boy here, right?" Roberta spoke in a choked voice.

"Right," I agreed.

The sound of something heavy falling hit against my ears.

"Roberta, you okay?" I said.

Roberta gurgled and hung up on me.

"This meat loaf is perfectly delicious," Baba said. "I think it's got sauerkraut in it. Taste."

"It's time you and me had a talk," Patsy said as we cleaned up the supper dishes. "You're holding out on me, Nora. I feel it in my bones. I'm your sister, aren't I? Sisters don't have secrets from each other. It's against the laws of sisterhood."

"Sure they do," I said. "If we told each other everything, we'd hate each other. You'd beat up on me if I told you everything, and I might knock your retainer down your throat if you told me everything. There has to be something private in our lives."

A sudden thought gripped me. "But

there is something special, Patsy, something that happened to me Saturday night when you were in bed."

"Chuck Whipple made a date with you," Patsy said, eyes narrow and glittering. "He snuck back here to see me and you waylaid him and . . ."

"No. It's something much more important than that," I said. I had made up my mind to tell her and Baba at the same time.

"I bet it's about Mother," Patsy said.

"I'm not telling till Baba wakes up from her nap," I said. "Then I'll tell you both."

"Damn, damn, damn," Patsy cried. "I know you saw her!"

Patsy's face got beet red and she stamped her foot.

"Grow up!" I said. "Just get a grip and stop acting like a spoiled brat. This is grown-up stuff we're talking here. I don't want any more nonsense from you! This is serious. If you can't act responsible and get your head together, forget it. I'll deal with it myself!"

Patsy's open mouth snapped shut. She

shuddered and said meekly, "You're right, Nora. I'm sorry. I'll be good," as if she was a small child again.

I had not expected Patsy to behave in this fashion. I was in shock. I was also, I realized with a pang, in control.

Nineteen

ONE THING about Baba, she's a good listener. She never interrupted once. Patsy did, a few times. Finally, after the third time, I just stopped talking and she got the idea and shut up. I told them everything, about me sitting in the dark, hearing the couch cushions sigh and having my hand taken and feeling a terrible cold creep up my arm. Even as I said these things, I thought, This is truly bizarre. They won't believe me.

"She was there," I said. "I know she was."

"How long ago, Nora?" Patsy wanted to know.

"The night I woke you up and asked

you what the other reason was that Daddy wanted to marry The Tooth," I said.

"You dog," Patsy said. "I wish you'd told me right then. You should've told me. If it'd been me, I would've told you."

Baba only nodded now and then and made little clicking sounds a few times, but she didn't say a word.

She never once said, "Oh, you must have imagined it, Nora." Never once. She only said when I'd finished, "Oh, how I wish I'd been there. How wonderful for you, Nora. Poor old Sam. I wish he'd been able to recognize that your mother had come back. It might make him feel better. He's on the horns of a dilemma. He knows you dislike Mrs. Ames and he wouldn't make you unhappy for anything in the world, but it *is* his life. Why not let him marry and be happy? Happi*er,* I should say. She's not a monster, is she? Your mother would want him to be happy. We know that much. So why not let him get on with his life? You two are getting older by the minute. Before you know it, you'll be off and running in the world. I'm not crazy about her either, but I say let Sam marry her and we'll make the best of it."

"That's easy for you to say," Patsy told Baba indignantly. "You don't live in this house and we do. I don't care if Daddy gets married, I only want him to marry someone nice, someone we like. Someone who likes us."

"Look at it this way," Baba said. "Imagine one of you bringing home a young man and telling your father this is the person you wanted to marry. And your father saying, 'I don't care if you fall in love, I only want you to fall in love with someone I approve of and like, and I don't fancy this person of yours.' "

Patsy looked shocked. "Oh, Daddy would never do that," she said.

"What makes you so sure?" Baba said. "What would be so different from him saying that and what you two are saying right now?"

Baba had a point. I was willing to recognize that, even though I didn't much like it.

"But we are only children," Patsy said. "We don't know stuff about getting married to the right person and so on." I knew that when Patsy fell into her "we are only children" routine, it meant she felt cornered and wanted to change the subject. If anyone else called us children, Patsy would most likely blow them away.

"Since when are people of twelve and thirteen children?" Baba said crossly. "Thirteen is halfway to twenty-six. You consider yourselves grown-up—until you're expected to act like grown-ups, and then you turn and run." Baba shook her head. "It won't wash, kidlets," she said.

"I don't know about you guys," I said, "but I'm going to go sit in the living room and think awhile, see what happens."

After a brief conference, Baba and Patsy joined me. We gave Baba Daddy's big chair on account of her broken wrist and also because she was the oldest. The three of us sat there in the dark.

"If I brought somebody like Casey Fullum home to meet Daddy," Patsy said, out of the blue, "well, I can see how Daddy might freak out." Casey Fullum had greasy black hair slanted over his forehead and completely covering one eye, and a horrendous complexion. He wore black denim from head to toe and scruffy pointy-toed boots and smoked pot for breakfast. He was fifteen and still in the eighth grade.

Patsy and I got to giggling, thinking of various people we'd bring home to Daddy that would blow his mind.

"Please, girls," Baba said. "Quiet. Concentrate. We are thinking of your mother." Baba's voice came slow and dreamy in the dark. "We are sending her loving thoughts, telling her we miss her and hope she is at peace. Concentrate on that."

"This is sort of like a seance," Patsy said.

"Patsy, I beg you, quiet," Baba said.

We all fell silent, thinking our own

thoughts. Instead of thinking of Mother, I'm ashamed to say, I thought of bringing Chuck Whipple home to meet Daddy. He would be very polite and respectful. He would shake Daddy's hand and maybe even call him "sir." Although maybe they don't call people "sir" in Iowa. They sure don't in Connecticut. Chuck would most likely blush, but otherwise he'd be cool. And Daddy would like him as much as I did.

Presently, we heard the garage door opening. It was Daddy. We stayed where we were.

"Anybody home?" Daddy called.

"We're in here, Sam," Baba said.

"Well." Daddy stood in the doorway and looked in at us sitting there in the dark.

"I thought I paid the electric bill, but I can see I was mistaken," he said. "What gives?"

"We just like sitting in the dark," I said.

"Sam, sit down, relax for a minute," Baba said. "You must be tired after your long day."

"I am, somewhat," Daddy said.

Baba reached over and turned on the light. Patsy and I blinked.

"Sam," Baba said, "Nora has something to tell you. I wish you'd listen and keep an open mind."

"Mrs. Ames called and said she has to go to San Francisco tomorrow and then to Hong Kong, so your trip will have to be postponed," I said, trying not to smile.

Daddy scowled and said, "Is she calling back?"

"No," I said. "I don't think so."

The telephone rang.

"I'll get it in the kitchen," Daddy said. "Maybe that's Wynne."

"It's either Roberta or The Tooth," I said. And either way, I thought, it's bound to be bad news.

Twenty

Instead, it turned out to be Dee Dulin. She was bringing Mother's portrait back on Friday, if that suited us. Her show was over and the gallery wanted everything out by the weekend.

"I asked her to stay for dinner," Daddy said. "Maybe you could call Glorious Grub and order one of their casseroles, Baba. That chicken thing is pretty good, as I recall. Now Nora, was there something else you wanted to tell me?"

I decided not to tell Daddy about seeing Mother's ghost. And hoped Patsy or Baba wouldn't tell him. For now, anyway. He wasn't in the right frame of mind.

Maybe he never would be.

"Mrs. Ames called and said she had to go to San Francisco," I said.

He nodded. "You told me. And then she's going on to Hong Kong. So our trip will have to be postponed. Does that make you happy?"

I was so surprised at his question, I blurted, "Did you ask her to marry you yet?"

"That's hardly an answer to my question, Nora," Daddy said. "But no, I haven't asked her yet. If I wait too long, she may think it's because I don't want her to be my wife because my daughters are opposed to the idea. It is very hard to please all of you. If not impossible. Now, if you'll excuse me, I'm going out to get myself a glass of milk."

I almost never fight with my father. We usually get along very well. Patsy and he sometimes fight, mainly because she's so fresh and thinks she should be allowed to do things that older kids can do, like go to the concert over in Stamford with Chuck Whipple, which she wasn't allowed to do.

He'd asked her before he met me. That was the first time I'd thought that. It made me smile.

I followed Daddy out to the kitchen. I wanted to be friends with him. We had always loved and respected each other. I didn't want that to change, and it seemed to me there was a good chance it would if he got married.

He was sitting at the table drinking a glass of chocolate milk. His dark eyes looked black in the overhead light.

When I sat down across from him, he looked at me, through me.

"Things are rough, Nora," he said. "I'm doing my best, and that's not good enough. Our world, yours and Patsy's and mine, fell apart when your mother died. But together I thought we could put it together again. It doesn't seem as if we're doing a very good job of it, though."

He shrugged and polished off his milk.

"You're a good child. I'm proud of you and of Patsy. Your mother is, too. I know that. How could she not be?"

I went over and sat on his lap. It was very uncomfortable sitting there. I was too tall, my neck was too long, there was no place to tuck my head. I was not a little girl. My legs dangled, and my sharp knees stuck out like two pieces of old bone. I was too big to be sitting on my father's lap. Still, I didn't know how to get off without embarrassing him and me, so I stayed there, not knowing what to say.

"It'll work out, Nora," Daddy said after a long silence. "We'll work it out together, the three of us."

I had a crick in my neck from bending my head at an odd angle. I got up from Daddy's lap at last and said, "I'd better go take a bath, Daddy."

"Yes," he said, "I guess you had better. Good night, darling. Thank you."

Thank me for what? I wondered as I climbed the stairs. What was he thanking me for? What had I done?

Twenty-one

WHEN I WENT to the library the next day, I planned on checking the computer for ghost books when I thought I heard a familiar voice.

"Hey, Nora. I didn't know you came here." It was Chuck Whipple and his brother, the one I'd met at the dinner theater.

"Sure, I come here all the time," I said.

"So. You're a reader," Chuck's brother said. "You look like a reader."

"Thanks," I said idiotically. Was that good or bad? I didn't even have my glasses on. Probably he meant I looked intellectual. I've been told I look intellectual several times. I never know how to take it. Is it a compliment or a put-down?

"Where's your girlfriend?" I said to Chuck's brother. Just for something to say. I should know by now that the things you say just for something to say are better left unsaid. Far better to keep your trap shut and give it the old Mona Lisa treatment, an enigmatic smile. That confuses them and gives you the upper hand. I read that somewhere and find it to be true.

Chuck's brother looked startled, then he blushed and said, "She left. Went home."

"Do they let you take out movies for nothing or do you have to pay?" Chuck asked me.

"Oh, they don't cost anything, but you have to take good care of them and make sure they're rewound right," I said. "You can have them for two days. There's a list of all the ones they have over there, on that big table."

"Thanks," Chuck said. He and his brother wandered off.

Hey, come back, I imagined myself calling to him. I want to kiss you. Last time I saw you, I was going to give you a major kiss, one you wouldn't forget in a hurry. Then Patsy showed up and ruined everything.

I said nothing, of course, and fooled around, looking at some books and newspapers, stalling. Keeping an eye on Chuck. Maybe I'd sound Chuck out about ghosts, see what his reaction was. See if he laughed or took the idea seriously.

When I saw Chuck and his brother leave, I waited a minute, then I left, too. Chuck was waiting outside for me.

"Where's your brother?" I said.

"Oh, he went on ahead," Chuck said. "He's in a bad mood. He had a huge fight with my folks because they wouldn't let him and his girl bunk in the same room. My mother said it was her house and he'd have to abide by the rules or leave. So then he called her a hypocrite and my father, who usually stays neutral in these things, got sore and said by God, it was his house, too, and what my mother says goes. Then Lauren got all uptight and hopped on the next bus to Maine, where she lives. Then my brother got sore at me when you asked him where his girlfriend was because he thought that meant I'd told you the whole story."

"Oh, boy," I said. "Families."

"You said it," Chuck said.

We walked a ways before I said, "I was looking for some books on ghosts in the library."

"Yeah?" Chuck said, "Any luck?"

"Not really," I said. "You see, I've kind of got a thing about ghosts. A couple of times I felt as if my mother was there. Her spirit, anyway." I laughed, but not because I thought it was amusing. "Have you ever had any experience, ghostwise?" I asked Chuck.

"We had a dog named Colonel," Chuck said. "He got killed by a truck. My dad dug a pretty deep grave out back and we buried Colonel in it. It was very sad. We all cried. Colonel was a big dog. We buried him deep so the other animals couldn't dig him up. We all said a prayer."

"I'm sorry," I said, as if Chuck was talking about a person who had died.

"So after that," Chuck continued, "I saw Colonel running down the road. Sometimes he raced alongside the school bus, the way he'd always done. When I got off the bus, I called and called, but he didn't come. Then, once, I looked out my window at night and I saw him running in the moonlight. So I put on my jacket and boots—there was snow on the ground—and went out to see if I could find him. But I never did."

"How could you be sure it was Colonel?" I said. "Maybe it was just a dog. Did he leave paw prints?"

Chuck shrugged. "I didn't notice. He wore his red collar with the tags dangling. No other dog I knew had a red collar."

"You mean you could actually *see* him running, *see* his collar?" I laughed again, but I felt embarrassed. It never occurred to me that animals could be ghosts. But why not?

"Sure," Chuck said. "Clear as day. Did you ever see your mother?"

I shook my head. "I felt her presence, even heard her laugh. Maybe I will see her sometime."

"Do you *want* to see her?" Chuck asked me.

"Well, I'm not sure. I sort of do and I sort of don't. I mean, I might be scared."

"I don't think you'd be scared," Chuck said, matter of factly. "I wasn't scared when I saw Colonel. I just felt happy."

"No offense," I said, "but I'm talking about my mother here, not my dog."

"I didn't mean to say they were the same thing," Chuck said. "All I meant was, if you actually *saw* your mother, I think it might make you feel better. That's all."

If I saw her, I thought but did not say, not trusting my voice to remain steady, I would want to see her the way she was before she got sick. Not after. Oh no, not after, I couldn't bear to see her that way.

"Sometime, when you're lying awake,

you can't sleep," Chuck said, "try to picture the way your mother would look, the clothes she'd be wearing. Did she have special clothes you liked? Or how she smelled. Colonel smelled like a musty old dog blanket he always slept on."

"My mother smelled of her favorite perfume. Shalimar," I said. "And I would like her to be wearing her taffeta dress. It was a beautiful, very noisy dress. You know the sound taffeta makes? It rustles, kind of snaps and crackles, so you could hear her coming before you saw her."

Chuck shook his head. "I never heard of a noisy dress," he said, "but it sounds okay."

"Or maybe she'd have on her old khaki shorts and her sweatshirt," I went on, intrigued by the idea of what my mother would be wearing when and if I saw her.

"And probably her sneakers. The ones with holes in the toes."

"Yeah, I know about those." We looked at Chuck's feet. Both his sneakers had holes in the toes.

We laughed as if he'd said something hilarious. He put his hand on my shoulder. I felt it resting there and thought in amazement, Why, I'm happy. Right this minute, I'm totally happy.

It was the first time since Mother had died. I hoped she would understand and not mind.

Twenty-two

FRIDAY was a school holiday on account of all our teachers had to go to a teachers' convention in Hartford. It was raining cats and dogs, so I decided to clean out my bureau drawers.

Patsy was flat out on the floor doing her leg lifts to firm her thighs. "Man, this is hard work," she panted. "Wonder how Jane Fonda hung in there so long."

"She was making money," I said. "And you're not."

Patsy sat up. "Why don't we rent a video camera and you can take shots of me doing leg lifts plus a couple one-arm push-ups, and we could sell it to a TV station that would pay me megabucks. That sounds cool."

The telephone rang, and I stepped over Patsy and went into Daddy's room to answer.

"Hi, Nora, it's Chuck," Chuck said. "I want to ask you something."

"Oh, hi, Chuck," I said, surprised. As if he was the last person in the world I expected to call.

In a flash Patsy was at my side, hand out, fingers snapping. Like the other time.

"He wants to speak to me," I said. But she grabbed the phone from me and started talking to Chuck. I was so mad I had spots in front of my eyes. I could feel the blood pounding in my head. I looked at myself in the mirror on the closet door. Two big spots of red in my cheeks looked as if they'd been painted on. I felt thorny and mean and ready to fight for my rights. A new feeling for me and not unpleasant.

I went down to the kitchen to get a big plastic bag to hold all the old T-shirts and shorts and stuff that I planned on chucking. Interesting choice of word. Patsy was at my heels. She turned on the radio and started rocking and bopping to the music that blared suddenly. I turned the radio off and said, "That was very rude, you know. Chuck wanted to ask me something and you grabbed the receiver before he had a chance. That's the second time you did that. It better be the last!"

"Why didn't you tell me to buzz off?" Patsy said. "Anyway, he was just being polite. He's a very polite dude, in case you didn't notice."

She flipped the radio back on. I promptly turned it off.

"What's with you?" she said. "Go get your own boyfriend. We don't have to share everything, you know, just because we're sisters."

"I'm the oldest," I said, idiotically, as if that made any difference.

"Yeah, that and thirty-five cents'll get you a Mars Bar," Patsy said, sticking her face right up to mine.

In your face. I hate that expression, but this time it fit. Patsy was in my face.

As if I'd planned it, I reached out and raked my fingernails, which were pretty long, along her arm. We stood there, watching, as blood spurted and tiny narrow red lines, like little railroad tracks, traveled down her bare skin.

"What'd you do *that* for?" Patsy cried. "You're crazy, Nora. I'm telling Daddy!"

"Give up that telling Daddy routine," I said calmly. I wet a wad of paper towel. "Here," I said. "Wash it off. I don't think you'll need stitches. Be brave. Chin up, kid." In a voice that seemed to come from someone else, I said, "You had it coming and you know it."

I went upstairs and filled the plastic bag until it bulged. I planned on taking it down to the bin at the A&P when it stopped raining. The same bin we'd put The Tooth's stuff in.

The telephone rang again. No one answered. It rang about ten times. Patsy must have gone out. Either that or she was bleeding to death. I went into Daddy's room and picked it up.

"Hey, Nora," Chuck said. "Patsy said you'd call me back."

"She must've forgotten," I said.

"What I wanted to ask you was if you could go to Radio City Music Hall with my parents and me."

I caught my breath. Was it a real date if his parents were along?

"My father has always wanted to go and my mother loves the Rockettes," Chuck told me. "They said I could ask a friend, so I'm asking you. We're taking the train into the city."

"When?" I said.

"A week from Saturday," Chuck said. I could tell he was excited. So was I. I know it's not cool to get excited, but I do, a lot.

"I'll have to ask my father, Chuck," I said. "I'll call you back. Daddy won't be home until late, so I'll let you know tomorrow. Is that okay?"

Maybe he'd ask someone else if Daddy said I couldn't go. I didn't even want to think about it.

"Sure, that's fine," he said.

So much for sharing.

Dee called to say she had a terrible cold and could she take a rain check on dinner.

"Sure," I said.

The minute I hung up, Patsy was at my side. She held out her arm, making a long face. I didn't tell her what Chuck had wanted.

"Say you're sorry," she said.

"*You* say *you're* sorry for being such a brat," I said.

Patsy surprised me by saying, "Okay, I'm sorry."

"I accept your apology," I said.

Long after I heard Daddy come home and the endless day had ended, I lay in bed, thinking about going to Radio City with Chuck. (I had decided it was a real date even if his parents came with us.)

Pale moonlight came in the window. The rain had stopped.

I hugged myself and thought of Mother.

I kept my eyes open, staring into the dark, hoping she might come. I was getting slightly loony on the subject, but ever since Chuck had told me about seeing his dog, the idea that I might actually *see* her had never left me.

I waited quite a long time, but nothing happened.

Twenty-three

PATSY WAS in a foul mood and had been ever since I told her Chuck had asked me to go to Radio City with his parents. She kept flipping out her retainer and grinning at me at the same time, and it was making me very nervous.

"What do they want to go to Radio City for?" she asked me. "That's totally uncool to go there."

"Not if you're from Iowa it isn't," I said.

"Is it black-tie?" Roberta asked.

Just to freak her out, I said, "Yes."

"You've got to be kidding me!" Roberta hollered.

"I might have to buy a gown," I said. The word *gown* always strikes me as being pretentious and silly.

"A gown." That really shook Roberta up. "How do you figure what's a gown and what's a dress?"

"I think a dress is plain and a gown has all kinds of stuff stuck on it. Like feathers and sequins and ruffles," I said.

"You're going to look pretty funny in a gown is all I can say," Roberta said.

"Maybe I'll just wear a black tie and call it quits," I said.

Roberta hung up in a huff. She has no sense of humor sometimes.

Baba went with me to pick out a dress to wear. Her wrist was better, but Dee drove us downtown.

"Midwesterners often think of easterners as rather flamboyant," Baba said. "Nothing wrong with a little flamboyance, I always say. But for a young girl going to New York with a young man and his parents, I think we should aim for moderation. Nothing in orange silk with holes cut out back and front. No silver leather shorts. Something pretty would be nice."

"Black is in," I said.

"Black is for sex symbols and widows," Baba said.

"One out of two ain't bad," I reminded her.

We settled on a blue-and-white silk print with a wide white linen collar.

"*Little House on the Prairie,* baby," Patsy said. "All you need now is a sunbonnet."

I thought it looked like something Elizabeth Taylor would wear to a wedding. (Not one of her own—someone else's.) It was a demure dress with a certain amount of sex appeal.

Baba calls sex appeal *Oomph.* Which sounds to me like what you say when someone sticks their elbow into your stomach by mistake.

OOMPH!

Patsy offered to cut my hair.

"No thanks," I said. I wasn't taking any chances.

Now if only I didn't get diarrhea.

"How about if you get diarrhea?" Roberta asked me. "You know how you are."

I didn't even want to think about it.

Twenty-four

"YOU LOOK LOVELY, darling," Baba said. "Doesn't she, Sam?"

"What's all this commotion about?" Daddy looked over the top of his paper.

"This is the day Nora's going to Radio City with Chuck Whipple and his parents," Baba reminded Daddy. "They called and invited her, Sam, and we said it was fine. And Sam, it's none of my business, but don't you think you should shave? They'll be here any minute."

"I never shave on Saturday if I can help it," Daddy said. "Besides, I'm not going to Radio City, Nora is."

"What time is it?" I said.

"Nine–thirty-two," Patsy said. "Time for one more pit stop."

I shot into the bathroom. "If you ask me," I said, "this isn't worth it."

The doorbell rang.

"I'll get it," Daddy said.

I heard him say, "You must be Chuck. Come in, come in, young man. She's all set." He made it sound as if I'd been suited up and ready to go for hours. Chuck had on a jacket and tie. I almost didn't recognize him.

Daddy introduced Chuck to Baba. She liked him right away, I could tell.

Patsy had disappeared. Probably she was hiding in the broom closet, spying on us.

"You can't go without any money, darling," Daddy told me. "You never know when you might need some, have to make a phone call or something."

"My father's paying for everything," Chuck said. Then he blushed a vivid red.

"Just in case." My father tucked a twenty-dollar bill into my hand. Luckily, my dress had pockets. I wasn't bothering with a purse. It might get ripped off.

"We'll be home about six, if that's okay," Chuck said. "If we're delayed, we'll call so you won't worry." I bet his stepmother told him to say that.

"Fine," Daddy said.

I gave him and Baba a quick kiss. I thought I heard Patsy rustling around in the broom closet. By now she was probably running out of oxygen in there.

"Nice to meet you," Chuck said, shaking my father's hand.

"Take good care of her," Baba said. I could've died.

Chuck ducked his head. "I sure will," he said.

Daddy walked out to the car with us. Chuck's father got out and shook my father's hand. Chuck's stepmother leaned out and shook hands with Daddy, too. It was like a bunch of heads of state meeting at the White House, all smiling and shaking hands.

Chuck and I got into the backseat and the door closed on us.

I had a mad urge to escape—holler "Help!" and run for my life. But I could barely move my lips. I might not be able to talk the whole day. The Whipples would think I was a moron. So would Chuck.

"We're so excited, Nora." Mrs. Whipple turned to look at me. "I haven't been to New York since I was about ten. We went to the automat and put in our nickels and got a slice of pie and hot chocolate. Oh, it was such fun. The food just popped out at us. I'd never seen such a thing."

"I don't think there are any automats left," I said.

"What a shame," Mrs. Whipple said.

"Fasten your seat belts, kids, and just remember, we all stick together," Chuck's father said. "I don't want anyone to get lost, myself included." I guess he was nervous, too.

It was going to be all right. The Whipples were easy to talk to. I began to relax a little.

We turned down Roberta's street. She

was standing on the sidewalk, waiting. I pretended I didn't see her.

"Hey, Nora!" Roberta shrieked. "Bon voyage! Don't do anything I wouldn't do!"

We sailed on by, and I'm happy to say I didn't so much as wave.

Twenty-five

WE WALKED UP Fifth Avenue. Nobody tried to rip us off until we went into a store with a big EVERYTHING MUST GO! sign on the window. Then we went into a bookstore, Saks Fifth Avenue, and St. Patrick's Cathedral. Chuck's father checked his watch and said we'd better hurry if we wanted lunch. He'd made a reservation at a restaurant that looked over the Rockefeller Center skating rink. When I saw the menu, I was glad I'd brought the twenty dollars Daddy had given me. Mr. Whipple might need it to pay the bill, I thought.

I had the chicken salad. The others had hamburgers. Mrs. Whipple asked the waitress where the ladies' room was. I went with her.

"I always like to go to the ladies' room in a strange place," she told me. Right away that made me like her more.

"So do I," I said.

"Chuck's dad and I are so glad you are friends," his stepmother said. "It's tough being a stranger in a strange place."

"Well, I like him," I said.

She smiled. "So do I," she said. "He's a lovely boy. If he were my own, I couldn't love him more. He has a kind heart. A kind heart is a great gift. I think he must've inherited it from his mother."

When we got to the theater, Mr. Whipple gave Chuck two tickets. "I wasn't about to get four seats together," he said, "so we'll have to split up and sit two and two." Chuck and I sat four rows behind his parents. I was glad. That made it seem more like a real date on our own, just the two of us.

"Are you all right?" Chuck asked me.

"Sure," I said. "I'm fine. Once our mother brought us here and Patsy and I saw a very scary movie, so we watched through the holes in our straw hats. It wasn't nearly as scary that way."

"You're funny." He took my hand. "Just so you don't get lost," he said. We both laughed.

"So are you," I said.

"I made the basketball team," he said. "Not first string. The coach says I'll have to practice a lot, but I might get good enough."

"That's excellent, really excellent," I said. "Good for you."

We looked at each other in the half darkness. His face was very close to mine. He smelled of soap and water. I'm glad his ears are big. If they weren't, he'd be too handsome. I wanted to touch his smooth cheek, but I figured I didn't know him well enough. Probably he didn't have to shave yet.

The lights dimmed and the show began. Some singer imitated Frank Sinatra and Bob Dylan. The Rockettes were better. They were truly astonishing with those legs all kicking in unison. I planned to try that with Patsy when I got home.

We split a Mounds Bar. I felt very happy as I bit into the coconut. I thought I might be in love, although I wasn't sure what being in love felt like. My insides felt exhilarated and my heart thumped so noisily I wondered if he could hear it.

After, we stopped for a Coke. I wanted to say this was my treat and whip out my twenty-dollar bill, but I didn't have the nerve. Besides, I didn't know how much tip to leave.

We walked slowly through the dusk to the station. The buildings looked like black paper cutouts against the peach-colored sky.

"I can't imagine anyone saying New York is a horrible place," Mrs. Whipple said. "It seems to me quite wonderful."

Her foot hit what looked like a bundle of rags lying in a doorway. The bundle sat up and eyes looked out of it, straight at us. A guttural voice said something, a hand crept out from the rags, palm up. "I'm hungry," the voice rasped. "Please help me."

My hand went into my pocket and

closed around the twenty-dollar bill. I handed it to the bundle of rags.

"Oh, thank you, thank you," the voice said.

We walked on. No one said a word. Just as we rounded the corner to Grand Central, a man came running toward us. We crossed to the opposite side of the street. It was just a running man. He meant no harm. But we shrank against what he might have planned for us.

On the train Chuck said to me, "That was a good deed, handing over your money." I shrugged, giddy with pleasure at his compliment. I hoped he thought I did good deeds like that every day of my life.

We drove home slowly through the dark streets. I wanted the day to never end, to just go on and on. The Whipples let us out at my street corner. Chuck said he'd walk me home.

"Thank you for a wonderful time," I said. "I will always remember what a lovely time it was."

"We loved having you, Nora," Mrs. Whipple said.

"Be sure you see Nora to the door," Mr. Whipple told Chuck.

We walked as slowly as it was possible to walk without coming to a standstill. Chuck took my hand and we swung along together.

I had made up my mind. I would kiss him. It was to be a friendly kiss, straightforward. Not a big spitty kiss, with my mouth open and smushing saliva all around, the way they do on TV and in the movies. It wouldn't be that kind of kiss.

"Thank you for a wonderful time," I said. We were almost at my door. I think the curtains in the living room moved. Patsy.

The heck with Patsy.

I love you, I thought but did not say. I let the words run through my mind. *I love you.*

I thought of my mother playing Spin the Bottle and grabbing the boys and kissing them until she felt like letting go. Good for her.

I turned to him and put my mouth on his and kept my eyes open. I wanted to look at Chuck when I kissed him. In those big spitty kisses they always close their eyes. I never could figure that out. Why did they close their eyes?

He jumped a little, then kissed me back. His eyes were open, too. Our eyeballs were practically touching. I couldn't help laughing. It was so funny. Chuck laughed, too.

It was a marvelous feeling, laughing with someone you'd just kissed. It was my first kiss. I loved him. Well, make that *liked. Love* is a powerful word you have to think a lot about before you say it.

I stood there after Chuck had gone, thinking about my father, hoping he liked Chuck. I would feel terrible if he didn't like him.

"How was it?" Patsy pounced.

"Good," I said. "We had a good time."

"Did he put the moves on you?"

"No," I said.

"I guess those guys from Iowa are pretty slow," Patsy said.

I smiled to myself. I had put the moves on *him*. I grabbed him and kissed him, and he didn't even struggle.

On Sunday morning I woke up early, before anyone else. The sun was up and shining, and spring was just around the corner, I figured. It was a lovely day and I stood at the open door—looking out and taking deep breaths—and thought about kissing Chuck yesterday. Maybe I should've waited. Maybe I should've let him make the first move. Maybe he wouldn't have made any move.

I wondered if Chuck would tell the other kids what I'd done. Then they'd blow it up and make a really weird story about what had happened. Spread it all around school.

Heck with it. I wasn't going to brood.

I decided to go over to Dee's studio, see if she was there. She works early in the

morning, seven days a week. If she was in-
volved in painting something, she might be
there.

If Dee looked spaced out when I
knocked, I'd know her juices were flowing
and she didn't want to be disturbed.

Today I hit it right. She had just put the
finishing touches on a portrait of a mother
with her arms encircling two little children.
All three had dark hair and widely spaced
dark eyes. They were very beautiful.

"Oh, Dee," I said. She grinned.

"Yeah, it's good, right? This captures
them. This lives and breathes. It's good. I'm
thrilled with it. What's up, Nora? You hungry? Thirsty? Both? Sit and I'll fetch some
goodies. If I have any. Yeah, I think I do."

She brought forth a turquoise teapot
decorated with yellow dragons. We had Or-
eos and tea with a plastic container of milk
and Cheerios. It was a feast.

"Talk to me," Dee commanded. "I
haven't talked to a living soul for days.
How's everything going?"

"Remember a long time ago when Patsy stubbed her toe and we laughed and I said I thought I heard Mother laughing with us?" I said.

"Has she been laughing again?" Dee said.

"No." I ate my way slowly around an Oreo. "But I think I felt her in my room one night. She kissed me." I swallowed. "And she was there another time, in the living room."

Dee nodded, listening.

"Some days I'm so sad my stomach hurts," I said. "I wonder if she's happy and free of pain. Sometimes I worry that even though she's dead, it still hurts. I can't forget the way she looked before she died."

"Nora, darling." Dee put out her hand but didn't touch me. "I think your mother, wherever she is, is happy and free of pain. And as lovely as ever. Her spirit remains. She is strong and full of love for you. That's what I think."

"Good," I said. "Thanks."

"How's your dad? And Patsy?"

"Okay. Daddy says he might marry The Tooth. Patsy's having fits."

"Don't let Patsy get you down, Nora." Dee poured more tea. "Don't let her walk all over you. She comes on pretty strong at times. She'll take over if you let her. You and Patsy are made from different cloth. Cookie?"

I shook my head, wanting her to go on.

"I don't know why, but Patsy has self-confidence to burn," Dee said. "And you don't, but you should." Dee cupped my chin in her hand. "You have the dearest little face, Nora. I can see your soul shining out of your eyes. I think you'll be a perfectly splendid woman and you'll do lots of good things."

"You do?" I whispered, overcome. "What?"

"You expect me to know *everything?*" Dee cried. "Better scoot now. I have a major cleanup to do here and I don't need any help."

I knew she meant it. Dee liked to clean up on her own. I walked to the door and paused, wondering if I should tell her.

"Dee," I said, "I kissed Chuck Whipple on Saturday. He took me to Radio City Music Hall and on the way home I just grabbed hold of him and kissed him. He was surprised. I grabbed him, he didn't grab me."

"Was it fun?" Dee asked me.

"Yes," I said. "I liked it. I couldn't believe I really did it. I just grabbed him and kissed him."

"Good for you, Nora!" Dee said. "You're your mother's own daughter, all right."

I walked home slowly, thinking about what Dee had said. And of all the comforting things she'd told me, those last words were the best of all.

Twenty-six

THE TOOTH is back. She came back a week early. I heard Daddy making a date with her on the phone. His voice sounded light and happy and delighted to be talking to her. It feels odd to have your father going on dates. I wonder if they go dutch or if he pays for everything.

Daddy said he liked Chuck and that he seemed like a good kid. Baba said she thought Chuck had lovely manners. Baba is really into manners. I was glad they liked him. And I realized I'd never said anything nice to Daddy about The Tooth.

"What's there to say?" Patsy asked.

Patsy's a sore loser. When I told her about The Tooth getting back early and calling Daddy for a date, she groaned and said, "There goes the ball game. Prepare for the worst."

Patsy is sometimes psychic.

About ten days after The Tooth got back, Daddy told us they were getting married the end of May.

"It will be a small wedding, family and close friends," he said. Then, looking straight at me, he said, "Wynne and I would like you two to be members of the wedding."

"You mean bridesmaids?" Patsy yelped. Funny thing, she has always wanted to be a bridesmaid, though not—God forbid—a bride.

Daddy laughed. I hadn't heard him laugh in a long time, I thought, and it was a nice sound.

"No, I think not, Patsy," he said. "Maybe you could just stand up with us to show goodwill and that you wish us happiness. How would that be?"

We said okay.

That night as Patsy was putting lavender gunk on her face to give herself a facial and clear her skin of impurities, she said, "I see us in pink *frocks* and carrying bouquets of sweetheart roses. What say, Norrie? Does that sound good?"

"You heard Daddy," I said. "No bridesmaids."

"Yeah, but listen," Patsy said. "As The Tooth comes down the aisle, we trip her up and she lands splat and breaks lots of bones, and they haul her off to the hospital where they put her in traction."

"They could still get married," I said. "One minute you won't go to the church and the next, you're a bridesmaid. Make up your mind."

"Or"—Patsy paused for her knockout blow—"or, we tuck a couple of black widow spiders in our bouquets and at the crucial moment, the spiders hop out and nail The Tooth and send her to Never-Never Land. How's that?"

Like I say, Patsy's a sore loser.

After Daddy told us his plans, I went over to Baba's to see what she thought.

"Wish them well, darling," Baba said. "Your father would do anything in the world for you two. But you can't expect him to throw her over just because you don't care for her. If he were that kind of man, he wouldn't be Sam. You really don't have any right to say who he should marry. It's out of your control. Give them your blessing, Nora," Baba said. "That's what he wants, more than anything."

The wedding reception would be at our house, Daddy told us. He'd get Glorious Grub to provide the food.

To show Daddy he had my blessing, I decided to clean the house for him. Cleaning house is not my idea of a fun time. It was a labor of love.

I got out the vacuum. Vacuuming's the best part. I like the humming sound the vacuum makes. It's very soothing.

First I did the living room rug. Then the couch. I used that special little attachment that gets down into the crevices. I was doing a thorough job when I felt something tucked among the cushions. I reached down and pulled out a white linen handkerchief. It smelled faintly of something familiar and very delicious.

Shalimar. My heart began to pound.

I'd know that smell anywhere.

It was Mother's handkerchief. She had put it there so she'd have an excuse to come back, like Louise said. It was a memento.

Or maybe a sign. Maybe a sign that this was the last time she'd come.

I wasn't sure, but I *was* sure she'd left it for me.

I'd tell Daddy and Patsy, of course. And Baba, too. But not right away. I'm going to keep it to myself for a while. Not long. Not forever.

But even when I tell them, it will be mine to keep.